Sweetener

ALSO BY MARISSA HIGGINS

A Good Happy Girl

Sweetener

A NOVEL

Marissa Higgins

CATAPULT
NEW YORK

Sweetener

Copyright © 2025 by Marissa Higgins

First Catapult edition: 2025

ISBN: 978-1-64622-257-5

Library of Congress Control Number: 2025931945

Jacket design by Sarah Brody
Jacket image © Shutterstock / Olga Lewska
Book design by Laura Berry

Catapult
New York, NY
books.catapult.co

Printed in the United States of America

1 3 5 7 9 10 8 6 4 2

For our changed lives

"break up with your girlfriend, i'm bored"
BY ARIANA GRANDE
PERFORMED BY LANA DEL REY,
BBC RADIO 1'S LIVE LOUNGE

"not a lot, just forever"
BY ADRIANNE LENKER

"imperfect for you (a capella)"
BY ARIANA GRANDE

I lied because I wanted to make myself
seem more interesting.
—LOLA, *Confessions of a Teenage Drama Queen* (2004)

Sweetener

Content Warnings

ALCOHOL / DRUG ABUSE

CHILD ABUSE / CSA

MENTAL HEALTH / SUICIDAL IDEATION

PREGNANCY / BIRTH

EXPLICIT SEX

Rebecca

PROLOGUE

MY BABY IS THE UGLIEST BABY ON THE BUS. WE get looks. Women tell themselves I should be lucky to have a baby, even an ugly one, looking the way I do. Sweat moves from my cleavage to my stomach. My good shirt is already damp at the core of my back. I didn't expect running to the bus to crack my salt water. The weight of a baby will do that, I guess.

My baby doesn't cry. It hasn't, yet. I want to tell the other mothers this: My baby is ugly but he's happy. I know what they're thinking: That baby isn't really hers. My baby and I are both ugly but they're right: We don't look alike. And why would we? Heads or Tails don't get us here; it's not going to make sense.

A woman chooses us over the empty seats beside men and sits down. Hi, she says to the baby, ignoring me. Hi. My ugly baby regards her with patience. My ugly baby doesn't howl or spit. I think: Wow. That's some serious self-control. The woman mimes patty-cake and the ugly baby watches her until the woman gives up. Not quite there yet, the woman says. I tell her we're working through a lot of trauma and the woman goes into herself, ashamed at her intrusion.

The woman exits two stops later and I face the baby. Hey, I say. Let's try. I explain to the baby that we're going to do what that weirdo tried but we'll make it worthwhile. The baby raises its eyebrow. If you grab my right hand, I tell the baby, we're going to get off at Rebecca's stop. If you grab my left hand, we're getting off at Charlotte's. The baby raises its other eyebrow.

Come on, I say. You're too little to toss a nickel.

The baby smacks both sides of my face and laughs. It's like the coin landed on its side; no good. I tweak the baby's nose and it looks surprised. It occurs to me no one has ever been mean to it and I wish I could remember how that feels, or if I've experienced that at all. The baby hesitates then wiggles its right hand and that's all I need. I tell it I'll be here forever, I won't ever ever leave, no matter what choices anyone makes. The baby headbutts me and I feel an insurmountable bliss.

1

SIX MONTHS AFTER REBECCA AND I SEPARATE, I hover outside an organic market on Wisconsin Ave., relieved and surprised. Though I've lived in D.C. for nearly three years, the streets and neighborhoods continue to evade me. Before I left my wife, I asked her to meet me at restaurants and stores with singular fronts; chains, even local ones, provided too much room for error. She called me her child, her little girl—at first, with love, then, as a joke in a tone that caused our friends to look away from us, unsettled, and then, finally, as words uttered without regarding me at all. In the days after I moved out of our studio, during the dead period between Christmas and New Year's, I returned to collect small necessities: a turtleneck her mother gifted me one birthday, the thickest one I owned; an electric heating pad; and two thick fists of tampons. With red eyes, she said she was surprised I found my way back. I admitted to her I was too.

As I left she advised me to take care of myself, to stop eating so much shit, to talk to somebody about all my big feelings. I told her to buy bananas and stop drinking so much. No, I didn't say those things—I thought them. She told me to come back over so we could talk. I said, Okay. Six months later, as the person I guess is the manager of the market rounds the corner, I wonder not for the first time if moving on is what my wife meant by taking care.

To avoid making eye contact too early, I home in on my phone and refresh my pinkest app. I count one two three, one two three, a little pattern I devised in hope that repetition makes money and affection more likely. Five messages appear, *hi baby how are you hey gorgeous you really gay or what*, and none are my wish-list women. I recheck my favorites tab to see if any potential sugar mamas are missing. Women do that: drop. From my life and from my app of choice. They find other sweet girls, I guess. Or they give up. I skim my settings to make sure nothing has been reset. When I first made my account on the app, I let anyone see me and be seen by me. A mistake, as every time I was reminded of my wife by women with her traits—five feet six Virgo frequent drinking fluent in sarcasm mostly vegan—I numbed out. Fiddled with my brain's sense of space. Better, I reasoned, to block all reminders—at least until she serves me with divorce papers.

On the street, I look up and the manager has headphones in and a sunken line of a mouth. Her face, like my own, whispers a hangover. I tap over to my profile and browse my own photos, as my areolas settle me faster than counting my breaths. I want to remind myself I have a body. I'd put real hours into that profile, turning and twisting my torso, timing my shifts at the organic market so I could be home for a good morning light. With so many seekers and so few providers, I could not be lazy. When the approaching woman stumbles over uneven sidewalk and curses, I am convinced she will be in a bad mood, will screw me, and will let her bad moments ruin my life.

To feel powerful, I, for the first time, switch my profile from *seeker* to *provider*. I ready my face to appear likable enough to push and pull croissants from an oven. Trust me, I hope my face says. I understand temperamental layers.

The woman approaches and says, Hey. Rachel? She doesn't move to shake my hand. I rationalize this not as a slight but a matter of convenience because she holds a tall coffee and what appears to be a bagel from the convenience store I passed on my walk. She gives me a look, exhausted and a little confused, and I hope she's loaded that bread with meat, egg, and cheese.

I tell her no and give her my name though it hurts to say because it makes me miss my wife. My wife and I have the same first name, though our friends never used mine; I've always been Rebecca's wife, and in the time before her, I was addressed too rarely for it to matter. Our last names, too, are still the same, as I took hers at our court wedding. How funny and strange and odd. I repeat this line to myself, my little inner monologue building out a fantasy of what might happen if we're ever confronted over using the same social security number. With the same name, paperwork gets confusing. With the same name, it's easy to become one person instead of two.

She tells me she's had like, fifty applications for this one position. I shouldn't be surprised; I saw the bakery listing while I was prowling the break room bulletin board for extra shifts. The listing says it's just one morning shift a week but the pay is five dollars more per hour than what I make scanning and bagging. I'd eat her out to get this gig.

No worries, I tell her. I have one of those faces. She laughs and I love her a little. A woman and a kid walk by, bleary-eyed and pleasant. The woman squints at the hours of operation on the glass doors; the market, including the bakery and café nestled inside, doesn't open for another hour. As the manager unlocks the front door, I turn to watch the woman yank up the waist of her leggings. I wonder if she's hoping for a baby to take up room there or anywhere else in her life.

Inside the market, I remind myself I am a person. I have an age, a birthday, an address. I make up hobbies, friends. Two enormous Pride flags hang in the bakery but I can't read the manager so I remind myself to stay neutral. She excuses herself and slips into the kitchen to, in her words, heat things up.

Nice and quiet, the manager says. Right? She's taken apart her bagel and spread the innards on a few white napkins.

Totally, I tell her. I love room to think. I can smell sharp cheddar and one or two kinds of meat. I wonder if she's added mustard or if she's gone full yuppie with an aioli. She has two forks going and individual components are lost to enthusiasm.

Right, she says. So you'll do prep work in the back, she says. Not the register, unless we're slammed. You already knew that from the ad, yeah?

I say, Yeah. I curve my shoulders forward and put my weight in my hips, causing my stomach to curl outward, in order to mimic her stance. I prepared for the interview by rehearsing the right ways to speak: Yes, ma'am, No, thank you, It's my pleasure, Thank you so much, Beautiful, beautiful air-conditioning, isn't it? In real life, at close to five thirty in the morning, I sense this manager would find such courtesy off-putting. I crack my lower back for effect. Within seconds, she does the same and lets out a grunt.

The manager's teeth, like my own, are a reliable give. Not just a little shifting from forgetting to wear a retainer in her twenties, but shifts and gaps and a missing molar on the left side. My teeth are alright at a glance, uniform enough, but thin and weak, faded enamel and see-through bones. The bottom row is also jacked with gaps and overlaps. We both smile with our mouths closed. I ask how long she's worked here and she tells me close to two years. She says she started on the register, then moved into bakery prep, then assistant manager, and now this. Fatigue and pride sit like partners in her voice. Ten minutes into the interview and she charms me enough that she's practically my blood, practically my only, practically everything I've got.

I tell her, Cool. I tell her it's a good sign when employees stick around and she nods, stepping back into herself, scoping me out. She remembers where we both stand in this game.

From an iPad, she reads bits of my application and I can tell it's the first time she's looked at it. She comments on how many times I've moved since college (western Massachusetts to Boston to New York to Portland (not the cool one in Oregon, the other one) to Durham (our only yard) to Atlanta (inexpensive New York) to Washington, D.C.) and wants to know why. I offer a partial truth: partner's jobs. Summer teaching gigs, two-classes-a-semester adjunct positions without health insurance or moving allowances. We sublet rooms listed on Craigslist and signed for them before seeing them in person. My wife and I loved risks then. Implicit to the manager, an untruth: that my wife is still my wife.

Cool, she says, disinterested. He works here now?

I go neutral, hope she picks up on my delicate language. Doctoral program, I say. So stable for at least a couple more years. Two lies in one shot: pretend my partner is a man and pretend his career still affects my life choices. Perhaps the latter impacted my life more than I want to admit.

Nice, she says. Speaking of doctors, they're not gonna let you up enough hours to go full-time and get health insurance. You good with that?

Sure, I say. Rebecca was the only one who had coverage

for years. When the flu hit us, she got antibiotics on the clinic's suspicion she carried a secondary bacterial condition. Within a day of filing the script, she was promising the pharmacy she lost the bottle in order to get a second dose for me. She really loved me then. I've joked that she'll be lucky if I don't wear her face into the hospital if I ever break a bone and she's transitioned from laughing to telling me to take care of my one small life. To the manager I add, Sounds great.

With that, she waves me to stand behind the register. We go over the requirements I read online: Shifts run 5:00 a.m. to 11:00 a.m., nonnegotiable. I'd work Sundays. Employees can switch shifts but they're at fault if no one shows up. No paid vacation days.

I say, Sweet. When she reaches for some hot sauce beneath the front counter, I ask when I would start, hoping to cement the notion that I'd receive the job. She nods, as though thinking, and squirts sauce on the last bit of bagel.

The person we hire can start in like, one week, she says. Without smiling she asks, Hobbies?

I say, Oh. I think: Making rent? I think: Getting myself off? I think: Finding a woman with more money than either of us to take me to the dentist? I focus on her eye bags and tell her, Sleep, offer up a little shrug. The manager calls me wise and finishes her sauced bagel in two large bites. Without wiping her hands, she shakes my hand. Together, our skin forms a damp seal. She tells me to grab something from the leftovers case. The girls are allowed to take things home when they close, she says. But sometimes they leave food for our openers.

Oh, I say. I really shouldn't. I'm not thinking of calories but of the disgust in my belly at this point in my menstrual cycle—prostaglandin bouncing around my body and throwing it off, or so says the internet, but I worry using this word will other me to the manager. And I don't know how to pronounce it. I tell her, Thanks, it all looks great.

She tells me the 6:00 a.m. crew will come and eat it right quick. I repeat my protest and she looks me hairline to ankles. I want to thank her for seeing a body in the space I hold and wonder how she might describe me. Mousy, meek. Posture of a shell. If I were to go missing, the police would use my email to figure out where I had last been. They'd come in, not buy a thing but accept free coffee, plenty of cream and sugar, the expensive kinds, full of fat and grace, and ask the manager all about me. I imagine her telling the cops, one man, one woman, that I didn't seem the type to get into that kind of shit. She'd recall I moved all over the place and they'd give up right quick, write me off as a woman who should have outgrown that funny business, and I'd be melding with dirt.

I'm good, I say. Promise. My eyes are on the slices of carrot cake, Rebecca's favorite.

Girl, the manager says. You serious? You're all bone.

I'm hormonal, I say. It's a whole thing. I hope she catches my careful consideration, my easy ability to blend and mirror her self, any self. I imagine her thinking: How smart! How quick! I imagine her feeling relief at the thought of this malleable, unhappy person working alongside the other poor, malleable, unhappy people

14

who arrange sprinkles. I hope she will not ask how I can possibly work without health insurance. Perhaps she, like my manager at my regular location, will assume my parents keep me on their plan, or that my partner foots the premium.

I GET MY wish, because she only pulls a banana chocolate chip muffin from the glass case, still without wiping her hands. Just take it, she says. They don't pay us enough. I thank her in three different ways—so much, seriously, and what a great morning—before I walk myself out. I glance back in to give her a wave, but she's already neck-deep into her iPad.

Outside, I make it two blocks to a corner and slip out of my shoes. Back against brick I devour the muffin and some of the brown paper, too. I taste grease and wonder if her bagel eggs were cooked in butter, spit, or oil. I give myself four minutes to aspire to happiness before I walk two miles to the other market for my shift. Hopeful for an endorphin hit, I check my app and see I have eighty-seven new messages. I say, Holy shit. Then I remember why.

2

YOUR FACE, CHARLOTTE, A CHILDLESS CLAYMATION artist living on the last year of her inheritance, says upon opening the apartment door. Her first and only sugar baby, a thirty-three-year-old doctoral student named Rebecca, is sitting on the bed she, as far as Charlotte knows, shared with her recently separated wife, Other Rebecca. I didn't think I'd see your smile again, Charlotte adds.

This Rebecca, who is sitting on the bed with Bea, a clingy rescue, all tongue and hunger, closes her laptop. Babe, she says. What? In her eyes: hope.

There were men, Charlotte says. Armed. She's trying her hardest to remember her lines, to make everything according to her partner's fantasy.

No, Rebecca says, appearing delighted. Where? Not at the register? But of course, they would be at the register. Unlike the regular supermarket down the street, the organic one doesn't cash checks or send money orders. Those are the needs of other sorts of people.

Charlotte raises her wrists and steps forward. Her Rebecca gasps and examines her skinny forearms; all her hair is upright, suspended as though in the cold, but no marks appear. Still, her Rebecca knows to imagine the rings of a metal handcuff or dry rope.

Was anyone shot, Rebecca breathes.

No, Charlotte says. It would have been impossible. She motions the drag of a knife to her throat. Her Rebecca holds her own jugular as though in solidarity. Charlotte pulls across her throat and her Rebecca smacks her hands away. Charlotte wants to enjoy this game, wants to remind herself where her loyalties lie—with this Rebecca, her Rebecca. Other Rebecca is fascinating, consumed online only. Pitiful, weird. Other Rebecca sounds cloying, a judgmental kid who never outgrew her shyness. Her Rebecca talks about her ex in increments tied to anecdotes: *she cried on the street trying to find this café, there's the bench where we breathed out a panic attack while her coworkers enjoyed a happy hour inside.* Charlotte nods, listens, recalls the photos of birthday dinners and wedding flowers, *love of my life, family of my life.*

The thought of your face, Charlotte says solemnly. It brought me home.

Bea, who Charlotte ignored upon letting herself inside, drops from her spot at the foot of the bed onto the floor. She watches the women begin to kiss. Turn around, Charlotte thinks. She considers arranging chew-toys in the tub to distract the dog, but she's afraid to rupture the fantasy. She finds herself thinking it's been a long time since she's felt so powerful, and as her Rebecca fake sobs, she wonders if the world can possibly continue to humor her demands.

How did you escape, her Rebecca says. How did you make it home to me?

Charlotte's favorite form of intimacy is fighting, but her second favorite is being fussed over. Surviving a hypothetical robbed-at-knifepoint mission feels old-fashioned and romantic, a story where all the women know their role. All that's missing is her pregnancy belly, the silicone stomach, a prop Rebecca said she was *okay* with when they started their arrangement and patently avoided ever since. The belly would add to the drama of this fantasy, if nothing else, and Charlotte has it in her mind that next time, she'll have a little pre-labor contraction scare . . .

I wore the rope down, Charlotte says. On the corner of the conveyor belt. Her Rebecca oohs approvingly and Charlotte proceeds to detail her fictional closing shift. The captors didn't do a great job tying up the workers, but they were good enough to keep people from escaping until they'd gotten into the back office. Charlotte admits she couldn't see inside the manager's office, but it was collectively understood the robbers were going for the safe. In Rebecca's apartment, Charlotte closes her eyes as though bringing an auditory memory back into focus: yes, an eerie voice—Other Rebecca, perhaps—telling the masked men to please be patient. Only two managers were on call, and one had locked themself into the unisex bathroom by the fish department. We can't keep doing this, Charlotte hears Other Rebecca say in her daydream. But in Rebecca's apartment, Charlotte isn't sure if she's found acceptance or simply walked down a dark dirt-lined tunnel.

Did the police take photos, her Rebecca says. Did they alert the community?

I left before all that, Charlotte says confidently, although this angle of questioning was new. I didn't want to waste a second. The women review Charlotte's brave escape while they have sex on the Rebeccas' bed. Charlotte goes down on Rebecca while sputtering about how she could have lost her, how she nearly didn't come home. Around the time Rebecca orgasms, she's talking about being an early widow. When she's done, she asks Charlotte if she wants to grab the vibrator drying by the bathroom sink.

No, she says. Charlotte doesn't have her belly on and she hardly wants to be touched. She wonders if this is what being a stone feels like, then reminds herself if she were a touch-me-not, she wouldn't feel so disappointed at being the vessel instead of the hull. Guilt knocks on her conscience while her Rebecca cuddles her from behind. This adoration is what she wanted, isn't it? She doesn't understand why this couldn't have all happened with her belly on. Why it couldn't be just fine.

Let me rub your back, her Rebecca says. Her hands are hot and moist on Charlotte's neck and she shudders. Her baby asks what Charlotte's been working on, how the art is going.

Charlotte stiffens, thinking about her bellies. She has

at least a dozen now, suspended in her walk-in closet. It started as bras, big beautiful ones, cups thick enough to support milk and pus and heartache. The straps suffered from the increased weight. The bellies are stiff, unyielding, empty—Charlotte papier-mâchéd them together, so the stomachs appear to sprout from all angles. In her sketches, Charlotte only needed to put her arms through two holes and her head up the middle, like a bulky sweater-vest. But the piece, inspired by Louise Bourgeois's *Avenza*, looks better without Charlotte. Braver, less exposed. She doesn't—can't—mention her spiders.

Something's missing, Charlotte admits. Her Rebecca doesn't ask what.

3

IN THE HOURS BEFORE MY FIRST FIFTEEN-MINUTE break, I feel holy scanning food. Gluten-free pizza crusts. Organic whole peeled tomatoes. Hot fudge in a glass jar, the prints of my dirty mitts a reminder I have not yet been replaced by a robot. Weekday mornings in an organic market offer few other surprises—just elders and agoraphobes and tickles from the other side of adulthood, nannies and toddlers and big organic grapefruits.

Regulars enter the store in the minutes we open, take to their carts, their aisles. I have been working here since just after I left Rebecca, working most of the same shifts on most of the same days. More than likely, I am part of customers' routines, though I don't believe I've ever impacted a person, not even and especially not myself. No significant talk, no rapport. Just a tired woman who looks a little too old to work a register but might be a graduate student. Might be working for some pocket money, if Mom and Dad finally gave her a talking to. They probably think I am one of those artists. Someone who walks up north from Dupont, where I would depart from my studio, a little redone attic, and take the long way to work. I would hover by Dumbarton Oaks to take pictures of flowers for my blog, a minor local sensation. To call my grandmother and tell her I love her. Yes, customers might think as I arrange their organic cheese crackers on top of their boxed low-sodium soups, Yes. An artist. That would explain the unhappiness in the cashier's posture. That, or the lack of a paid lunch hour.

The customers, of course, do not know about my morning messages. Some senders are familiar to me, from my hours spent scrolling the profiles of other women aspiring to be cared for. Their angled bellies and pert eyes fixed with happy surprise welcome me again, this time not as competition but as an opportunity. Compliments I have never before received—your earlobes are delicious, hiii this is weird but do you workout your calves a lot, I would love to be considered for the position of licking your kneecaps—sit in my inbox as I explain to a customer how to weigh organic nuts and dried berries. The bulk section does people in. Use what bag? Write down what number? What if I didn't look at the label, I just grabbed what delighted me? I hear people, of course. No one wants to do a little work when it's so comfortable to watch people below you sweat. Listening to management rarely gives me comfort but when it comes to loose berries and nuts, the rules win. No code, no weight, no purchase.

Really, the woman on the other side of my register says. You can't like, make up something? Her outfit is a monochrome fitness number. I think it is mauve or magenta but I can never remember which is which. I'll bet she bought it from a store that branded the color as desert sunset.

I tell her no. Each item from the bulk section has a different numerical code registered in the computer system. That code has the precise cost per ounce, including any sales at time of purchase. The woman looks down at her phone and back at me once, then twice, and huffs real deep so I know I am an inconvenience. When customers with crying babies face this struggle, I do pity them. When people share they're only shopping at this place because their rich boss demands it, I let them take the bag and go. Empathy might come easier if the woman were beautiful to me, which is a bad thought. A dirty thought. Wrong thought. But a thought. Her eyes reveal a sadness pressed behind a rage I believe is visible only to me. My eyes, I know, give off the same effect. I apologize to the woman, hoping it reduces the chances of her slamming my face into the conveyor belt.

She says, You don't know the number for like, I don't know. Peanuts? Cashews? She tugs at her sports bra and I notice a vomit stain down the front. I squint and wonder if bulimics are getting lazier or if she's hoping someone will notice and help. I tell myself to ease my tone with her, as she seems vulnerable either way.

We aren't advised to memorize the codes for the bulk section, I tell her. In my head, I'm already playing Heads or Tails; if she's understanding, it's Tails, and I just give them to her. I mention knowing the codes for the bananas. Bananas are so popular, I say. You could probably remember the code, too. If you wanted.

I don't want to remember the code, she tells me. I notice dried sweat below her hairline and wonder if she came from Pilates or spin or an early morning of both. She says, I'm not going to come back here if it's a literal *job* just to get my belongings.

I consider pointing out that nothing in this place yet belongs to her. Fluorescents, perhaps, may go beyond any ownership. Instead, I tell her she can go back to the bulk section, write down the code, and come back so I can weigh the little bags and cash her out. I apologize for the inconvenience, as I know that language works wonders on the upper class. It's Heads and she isn't getting shit.

When she tells me to go fuck myself, I smile. When she pushes by my bagger and exits the store, I pretend not to see my growing line of customers and dart away for my fifteen-minute break. I open my messages and read all the ways women want to do the work of fucking for me.

Fifteen minutes is tough. In twenty, I could lock myself in the bathroom, masturbate to messages, fingers on clitoris, wash my hands, piss, and eat a protein bar. At fifteen, the world closes up. I settle on eating two protein bars while I read. The second bar, I pound, of course, so I am full enough to be uncomfortable, to experience a pull inside my body I cannot repress. If I faint and crack my head against the register, I like to think I will get some kind of workers' compensation. I refuse to google and see if this assumption is legally sound.

Most messages are from women in their twenties. College students, graduate students, poorly paid interns who came to D.C. to work on the hill, unpaid interns who came to work the nonprofit sector. Because my profile is unchanged except for, perhaps, the most important part, the women reply to a narrative I intended to be read in reverse. In searching for a caretaker, I asked those who messaged me to describe their homes. I want to know: Homeowner? Roommate? Townhouse with the ex? With five male roommates of my own and two shared bathrooms, I will bring no creature back to my room. Even my wife does not know my street address, so intrinsic is my desire to leave no trace, to scuttle through the maze of my life like a rodent.

I don't respond to anyone but I read all the messages. Twice. I tell a coworker I can house-sit for some rich people for her and keep it quiet so she can go out of town with some girl. They have a jacuzzi, she texts. Perfect, I think, wondering if I'll finally feel alone enough to come.

Hours later, when my shift ends and the sun sits right in the sky, creating long shadows on cement and humidity enough to sleep in, I check my phone. Two messages get my attention. A reply from the user suggesting a number of cafés in ranked order based on my preferences on the app (lighting, neighborhood, vegetarian options, lack of live music). The user stressed that she didn't want me to feel pressured to accept her first suggestion; this is all about joy, she wrote. The second message is from my wife, and as a good partner, I, of course, open her message first. Her request sends me right back to when we were married—and reminds me that we haven't stopped. The text *Heads! I've solved our baby problem* will do that, I guess.

4

CHARLOTTE SCOOPS TOFU SCRAMBLE INTO THE paper boat. It's turmeric yellow with chopped spinach and broccoli and black olives. Charlotte scoops and scoops then adds two biscuits made with organic buttermilk. There's a lot of meat next to the tofu, hunks of grass-fed meatballs and turkey bacon patties. Eggs scrambled with sharp cheddar cheese and without. Olivia once wrote a twelve-page paper on the reasons she would never eat eggs again. Not for school, but for her parents, in an attempt to get them to stop forcing the treatment-approved protein into her gluten-free reduced-sugar waffle mix.

Charlotte can't see her friend from her spot at the hot bar, which is good for Olivia, who isn't supposed to look at calories on menus anymore, but better for Charlotte, who has suspended her scooping to study Other

Rebecca, who is tying a big apron around her waist and staring at the floor. Charlotte watches her nod while the woman typing into the register talks at her.

The numeral one lights up. So does Charlotte.

The Rebeccas don't look alike. Charlotte knew this from the photos her Rebecca kept of her wife around her apartment, as well as the social media reels. But it startles Charlotte to see this Rebecca on her own; in photos, the two of them leaned into each other, held hands, fed one another soup. In at least one video, Charlotte watched the Rebeccas sip from a coffee mug back and forth until the liquid drained. Last sip, the other Rebecca said. Last sip!! She faked it out like she'd finished it off, making her then girlfriend pout, but then made herself a hero and gave the first Rebecca the last drops. The women seemed to be two parts of a whole.

Charlotte imagined the other Rebecca to be sniffling, maybe, with a dirty sleeve up to her nose. But she looks just fine. Her eyes are small, as expected, but dark, like little puddles to the underworld. Charlotte, who is not a fan of working up a sweat, figures she could take this Rebecca if she had to. Like if Rebecca looked up over the register and said, Hey!, and somehow knew that Charlotte was sleeping with her wife and practically funding a baby she wouldn't ever meet, then Charlotte would get her to the ground until the police or at least until Rebecca came.

Behind the register, Other Rebecca seems even smaller. Her hair is fine and greasy at the scalp. Her eyes are like the marbles Charlotte sucked on as a child.

Charlotte isn't sure what her Rebecca sees in this one. Instead of tangling with the root of the thing—it's not about what lovers see in one another, but the depth of their shared language—Charlotte gets into line, her two allegedly compostable boxes stacked on top of each other.

The marbles transfixed me, she imagines telling her sugar baby. The round balls leaked into my brain and unraveled my simplest self: help, save, help save. She isn't sure which is which.

I understand, the Rebecca in her brain says. The marbles roll us into her soul.

Hi, Other Rebecca says, double-bagging paper bags. Did you get these from the hot bar or the cold bar? Her voice is high and mild, like a well-placed wind chime.

Look at me, Charlotte is thinking. Look. Charlotte wants to split Rebecca's eyes and extricate sand and glass and steel. She imagines milk seeds inside, like the kind found in the shit of a breastfed baby.

Ma'am, the other cashier says. Hot or cold? She points to the bar, where Charlotte notices a cluster of signs she'd ignored.

Both, Charlotte says confidently.

One hot, Other Rebecca says quickly. And one cold? She's evaluating the boxes like she might win a prize for guessing the correct weight. She hasn't looked at Charlotte, infuriating and delighting her.

They're both a combination, Charlotte says irritably, gesturing to the boxes to suggest that Rebecca open them, but she shakes her head no, face still to the floor. Charlotte considers leaving the food and running.

Can't mix 'em, different prices, the other cashier says flatly. Messes up our system. Charlotte wonders how many lesbians work in the market.

Charlotte stares. She has mastered the effectiveness of silence over her three decades of life. People will do much to avoid it, as she witnesses in her personal life, and also in customer-service situations. People will excuse a blank face if it's a pretty one. Especially if it's wet.

Charlotte begins to apologize with a cracked voice. She gets out *I* and *am* though not *sorry*. She doesn't care about the cost of the food. She will take a lifetime ban or a scolding. She covers her face with her hands to think. What will she do if Rebecca ever hears this story? Contact with her ex is a rule violation, albeit one that came on a generic template for sugaring she found online.

I don't know what to tell you, the other cashier says. I'm sorry but—

Pregnancy brain, Other Rebecca fills in, her voice hyper sweet. I can tell you won't be a repeat offender. From behind her fingers, Charlotte feels all four eyes on her stomach, the nice big belly she's swaying back and forth on her feet. Charlotte makes magic happen in her mind—an understanding moves through the women, relative strangers, that her belly does make her a good person, a sweet person, a person trying her best. A person who deserves just a little grace.

I HATE EGGS, Olivia says upon Charlotte's arrival to the market dining area.

It's the best tofu scramble I've ever had, Charlotte, who has eaten many a watery tofu scramble at small, dank artist retreats, continues. My mom and I love this nutritional yeast, you can actually buy it in bulk—

I can't believe *you* made me a plate of *your* favorite food, Olivia says.

It's really good, Charlotte says. Her heart is outside of her body, the extension of herself in a forbidden and already dulled place. I swear, she rambles, it's like, the *best*—

Charlotte, Olivia says seriously. You're a pill. Then she hunches face-first to both boxes.

The women share the food. Charlotte loves to share food even though it's undignified; her parents were strong proponents of the one-dish-at-a-time rule. The food bar feels comfortable to Charlotte, homey. She can scoop her buffalo tempeh on top of her mashed sweet potatoes. Swirl a little spaghetti around her crumbled soy. The world of the hot bar is an oyster, a balm to domestic bickering and marital disputes from simply sardonic to house-shushing.

Olivia takes to her desserts. Charlotte asks how the chocolate mousse is. She feels high off talking to Other Rebecca, giddy. A canary is singing somewhere in her stomach, beneath or beside the scrambled yellowed soy.

You made your perfect plate, Olivia says after some silence. You're either unbelievably self-centered or committed lifelong to the bit.

I'm your best friend, Charlotte says. I love you. She spider crawls across the table in her mind's eye and shoots a web around the souffle. Encouragement for you to eat, she says. Before the spiders get comfortable.

I like this place, Charlotte says seriously. Great sensory experience, high ceilings and French jazz. She is feeling weird. Curiosity isn't a crime, she reassures herself. The tofu tastes weird, now, which worries Charlotte—is this what depressed people feel like? It occurs to Charlotte that a little residential treatment could be nice. Lots of attention and rest, which Charlotte imagines as watching reality TV in a rec room. A few couches but most girls stretched on the floor. Popcorn with licorice, an elaborate sleepover with no boys, no phones, no distractions. Charlotte envisions herself analyzing behaviors displayed on-screen during commercial breaks, a self-assigned role that builds her self-esteem and resilience until she self-sabotages and gets stuck in her own web, a failure of the mother spider. She stops eating the tofu.

What's wrong, Olivia says. Did someone shit in the tofu?

Charlotte rolls her eyes. I lost my appetite, she says. She wants to tell Olivia about checking out at Rebecca's line, about how nice Rebecca was about her belly. How tingly it made her feel, reckless and mundane. But she hesitates; Rebecca talking to Charlotte would be one thing, but Charlotte initiating things is not likely to be received well. Especially after the great selfish plate debacle. Keeping a little secret from a tired and drained friend is noble, not selfish.

Talk to me about how you're feeling, Charlotte says. Olivia hates when people watch her eat, so Charlotte doesn't feel too guilty checking her app while her friend opens her soul.

I want to be weird, a new-to-Charlotte profile says. Less than one mile away. In the cafeteria market. While Olivia separates her spinach tomatoes, Charlotte whispers and sends a voice note: *I want to strap you to silk.*

5

OUTSIDE THE MARKET, I SIT AT THE BUS STOP, RE-
move my shoes, and rub my damp feet. I grab a plastic
gift card on the ground and type and retype the short
print on the back to see if there's money left—there is,
and I think this is a sign I should actually take a woman
out. I imagine ordering French toast after sex. I squeeze
the arch of my foot until I wince. There, I reason. I am
alive.

Cashiers are supposed to work in socks but I refuse,
a happy, easy rebellion. One less item to wash, one less
item to put away. Pairs add up, after all. In response to
the baby text, I message my wife: ??? I wonder if her message was old, an artifact of our relationship kept alive in
the draft folder. My spark of old hope is only a glitch in
the system.

The baby conversation feels dangerous, disorienting. I

used the possibility of a kid as an ultimatum for Rebecca to stop drinking, and the fallout was enormous; my wife quit alcohol on the spot then relapsed and tried to hide it (nips in her iced coffee on the way to class, off-campus happy hours when she knew I'd be at work) and I made the mistake of asking if the drinking was her way of communicating she'd changed her mind, about the child or about me. We never talked about what set her off—did she not know the answer, had I gotten too close to correct, or had the moon made our box studio appear unreal and therefore unsafe?—but when she ran, shoeless, from our unit, down the hallway, and out the front door to the district's midnight streets, I found the answer I needed. Even looking at a bruise can be too much pressure to bear.

I answer my wife's call midway through the second ring. I say, Hello? Divorced coworkers sometimes return calls from exes in the break room, voices ripe with irritation that could either reveal truth or cover wounds, I can never tell. With my wife, I feel too porous to pretend to be anything but hopeful and afraid.

Hi, she says. Thank you for answering. Her voice is the same one I hear when I replay old videos and voice memos about ordinary things. I tell her, Of course, and I wait. I pass an elderly couple splitting a sandwich on a bench. One cuts the bread with a plastic knife and the other grips the crust in both hands, both careful, careful. I don't want to cry on the phone and so I force myself to look at my own feet.

So, my wife says. I thought it would be easier to call

and talk about this. I'm sorry if my message wasn't clear. I tell her I am confused. She makes a noise to show she understands where I am coming from though she is about to disagree with me. She says, I know it's not fair for me to ask anything of you, but I'm serious about wanting to have a family.

I think: Family? My wife knows, I think, she is my only family. I want a sober Rebecca; I want my wife back. Me, this lonely weirdo. My parents were people before me, playful and messy—did they think my existence would keep them sober? The older I get, the more I resent their obtuse naivety in not aborting me, but also, the more I believe I am just as they are, as terrible and ignorant and wasteful, and that it wouldn't be hard for me to abandon or neglect a child. Me, this grown freak, the toddler that received no smiles. My wife makes me feel human, like a person worthy of patience.

I didn't know this would happen, I say on the phone. I realize I am crying. I think my wife and I aren't going into parenthood solid, not going in smart. I'm walking back to my little room, sweating and blubbering, my little nightmare of a space to sleep; I see her teaching at an old college in the city and I am taking her flowers on the ferry. The bouquet reminds me of children—roses, violets. Children; ours. Come home, she says. I do. I'm crying very hard

Oh, she says on the phone, in real life. Well.

I cry very hard. She says, It's still me, it's still me. It's me, it's me.

I go into my head to play Heads or Tails. I breathe

heavy with my eyes closed. The coin lifts into the dark; no one hears a drop.

She tells me the city views applicants on a rotating schedule, explains that there are all these mandated classes, and she wants to get moving sooner rather than later. Later, I guess, being after we actually get divorced. I ask her if she's still working the program and she says, Of course, fluid, patient, as though in the months before I left, she hadn't been telling anyone who suggested she cut back on the drinking to eat her shit. I want to believe her and so I tell her I don't know what to say.

I would love to adopt, she says. And I think we should talk about it. I think she asked me to marry her in the same way, though I can never remember, as the restaurant was so loud, and my excitement so bright.

I repeat, Adopt? She reminds me it was my idea. My wife is right; I suggested adoption over and over in the months she encouraged me to get pregnant. She enticed me in the usual ways: we already had names picked out, the baby would look so cute at our feet, everyone and especially her parents would take us more seriously. She would be nicer to me if I was pregnant. She'd drink less, she said, as total abstinence was not in our reality. Really, I asked her about that last one. You promise? Of course, she told me. Pregnancy changes everyone involved.

When I moved out a few months later, I expected her next baby news to come years later, that I would use a burner account to spy on her Facebook photos only to discover she had brought one home herself. Or that she moved back in with her mother to be doted upon. I ask her what I have to do with this now. I think of my twin bed and its broken springs. Despite myself, I think: Please speak in *we*. Speak in *us*.

I want to foster, she says, and my *Oh!* reveals too much, as I'm sure she desired.

We dated for close to eight months before I mentioned my childhood years spent in the system. I placed early. I was lucky to stay in a standalone house with a double yard, twenty minutes from the beach, the parents said, negotiating with me, I think, to stop screaming as the doors shut. With traffic, drives were close to thirty, but salt air and sunburn peels are all I remember with specificity from the years I lived with the parents I have not kept in touch with.

By sixth grade, my grandparents gained custody of me through a family-preferred placement in the courts. I thought they'd been trying the whole time, but by high school, I learned their appeal took only a few months once they filed papers. Oh, I thought. Oh. When it came to my wife wanting our own family, she at first wanted biology. Only blood. For years she repeated to me that there was nothing wrong with taking in someone else's child, but didn't I want one to look like us? I told her not really. Still, she said: Real family, real family. Blood. Without it, I suppose we did separate.

On the phone, I again ask her why she is telling me. I hope she is going to say she wants me to move back in. I understand none of my own wants, none of my own desires. I am living on instinct, gut, adrenaline. I resist thinking beyond the last time I woke up. And yet when she says she wants me to think about how important a family is to her, and what this could mean for her, I understand she is not using the word *we*. I say her name. I say, I don't understand my place in this. One of the few entirely honest things I've said in months.

The state does investigations, she says. Because we're still married, technically, I think it'll raise a ton of suspicion if you're not around.

Okay, I say. And you're sure it can't wait? I add, There are always kids waiting. I don't say what we both know, which is that the District requires a one-year separation before you can file papers for divorce. The separation begins when you stop cohabiting, and more specifically, when you stop sharing a bed. I signed the sublease for my room in the uniquely terrible days of early March, soggy and dark. I assume we will file papers on that date, though I am too afraid to ask. Instead, I add: Do you think we even make enough money?

I got some extra funding, she says quickly. In addition to my teaching stipend. I offer another *Oh* and she adds that the system really prefers to place kids in childless homes. Because we don't have any of our own, and we don't have records, I think we're a good fit.

Except it'll only be you, I say. Or are you thinking it'll be us on paper, and you raising the kid, or what? Kids talk, I continue. They'll mention it if I'm not even sleeping there. I am saying: Invite me home invite me home invite me home. Even more latent, I am thinking: If I want to go home, why did I leave? More latent: wine lips, whisky breath, overage fees. Chilled faces and dropped shoulders. I say, It's really important you're working the program. Kids will remember.

I am, she says. I hear more control in her voice than I expect. No anger, no snippiness. Still, her throat holds a secret, a superiority, a crack in the sidewalk for my sneaker to catch in. I wonder if her sponsor knows and what she thinks of it. I tell her I miss her and she says she misses me too. Then she says, So you'll come by when the social worker is here? It's like a consultation they do at your home.

I tell her, Okay. She says there are classes—we don't have to attend together, but we can. I tell her, Okay. Then she tells me to come by for dinner to talk about details, and I say, Oh, okay. I understand almost nothing, and so I respond to the last message I received; it's from a woman who lists herself as a *mommi seeking mommi* who is six years older than me and appears very close—less than a mile away. She sent a lot of texts I hadn't read. *Forget those places, meet me here in exactly 48 hours.* Her weird voice note makes me laugh, like I'm living all my life at once. I write Wait for me there—will make it if I can swing it xx.

6

CHARLOTTE FREEZES WHEN REBECCA ASKS HER IF she's having cramps; is that why she's touching her stomach so much? They're in the market where Rebecca's wife works, and Charlotte is hyped, wired. Can she get away with seeing Rebecca again? Nothing *should* happen; they're grown women in a supermarket, thinking about how much broccoli costs. But Charlotte wants Rebecca to fight her, to spring across that register, take her down and out.

Charlotte feels lonely without the belly. She's left it at home to keep Rebecca happy. I'm a little nervous, she says. Bad energy.

Nervous, Rebecca says. She looks at her seriously now, the way Charlotte is always wanting to be looked at.

She checked Other Rebecca's profile and saw she was up suspiciously early for a childless person with few responsibilities; she must be opening, Charlotte thinks. She's got to be here. She looked up how long grocery shifts were and was annoyed to find the average between four and nine hours. She considered calling the market but worried Rebecca herself would answer. This scenario terrified Charlotte because she both does and doesn't want to get caught sniffing around with wife number one. The thought makes her want to put her head beneath ice.

I think they use essential oils in this part of the store, Charlotte lies. Those fumes get me all turned around. If Rebecca notices smell sensitivities have never been an issue for Charlotte before, she doesn't mention it.

The women are standing in the flower section. Two men are in front of them in line, and Charlotte assumes they're buying bouquets for angry women. She and Rebecca listen to the men speak to the florist upon reaching the front desk. One man asks for good colors, lots of pinks, he specifies when pressed, and some of the little white flowers, too. He seems satisfied if disinterested by the bouquet he's given a few minutes later. The second man shows the worker something on his phone, and Charlotte finds herself insatiably curious. Was he thoughtful enough to save a photo of his woman's favorite flowers? The women listen. The worker slowly informs him that he's at the wrong place; that bouquet is actually a custom offering from another market, a mom-and-pop flower shop, up by the border of D.C. and Maryland. He huffs before leaving.

Charlotte is excited to impress the florist. She and Rebecca will not huff or argue. They'll know exactly what they want. The words *lesbian supremacy* cross her mind. She maintains a bright smile while the worker stares at the two of them like she's rewatching a commercial she's been able to recite since childhood.

Charlotte feels Rebecca looking around, glancing to and from the checkout lines, and feels jealous. She can imagine her Rebecca abandoning her, racing down the store to get to her wife, without once looking back. When Charlotte wants something very badly, she convinces herself that reality molds around her. According to her parents, this trait developed because she is an only child, a fact she cannot change.

I love houseplants, her Rebecca says. I'd live in a greenhouse if I could.

Charlotte says, Pick one, but Rebecca shakes her head and says they're so heavy, such a pain to move on foot. I have what I need, she says, and Charlotte smiles like she's found a stranger's secret.

Our little paradise, her Rebecca says, dreamy. Our big little bird-of-paradise.

Lilies, then, please, Charlotte says to the florist, thinking out loud. Can you do the lily of the valley surrounding the . . . tulips? The white. No, yes. Okay, but no baby's breath. Charlotte is thinking she's putting together a bohemian bridal bouquet, then feels sick wondering if the Rebeccas had bouquets at their wedding. Who wouldn't? She brings herself back into the wedding photos she'd seen around their apartment and online; were they yellow flowers? Orange? Out of season for a winter wedding, she remembered thinking. Just flowers, she tries to tell herself. Just living things that would die. But Charlotte has never been married, much less gay married, and feels sore about it. And the crocus, she adds. We love purple.

Sorry, Rebecca says, staring at her phone. I don't think we can do, um, any of those flowers.

Because they remind you of your wife, Charlotte blurts. For the first time, the worker leans in, engaged.

No, Rebecca says slowly. Because they're deadly to dogs. She looks pained.

Bea, Charlotte says. Bea becomes Pokey in her mind, Gumby's red pony companion. Be my friend, Charlotte thinks. Be my buddy.

What kind of dog is Bea, the worker asks. Rebecca says it's not a breed thing, the flowers are toxic, period, and Charlotte says Bea is a mutt.

She's a pit mix, Rebecca says quietly. Very shy.

You know what, Charlotte says slowly, and both women watch her face. They're wondering, she knows, what's going to come out of her mouth. Is she going to say something nasty about the dog? Is Bea overshadowing her role? Isn't she the one paying for the damn flowers? Charlotte pulls her mother up from the caverns of her development and uses her voice.

I'm really glad you mentioned Bea's needs, Charlotte tells Rebecca. You're so thoughtful. She turns to the worker. What flowers are safe for dogs? We'll go with whatever you recommend.

You want me to choose, the worker says slowly. She looks worried she's about to get yelled at, so Charlotte repeats her request with a bigger smile.

I can tell you have amazing taste, she says. I like, love your nose ring.

Before excusing herself to put a bouquet together, she warns the couple her taste is simple but her roommate has some big dog and he's never gotten sick from the flowers she's brought home. They last a while, the worker adds, her voice disembodied from behind a partially open door. Charlotte wonders if the other Rebecca ever sneaks back there and steals flowers; she can almost imagine Rebecca bringing home a single red rose, but she isn't sure if she wants to receive it or watch Rebecca give it to Rebecca. She rubs her stomach to self-soothe until Charlotte takes her hand and holds it.

Here she is, the worker says what feels like a long time later. Charlotte pulls out her wallet and tries not to look at the daffodils—her least favorite flower, if she's being honest—and that's when she notices the worker has another arm behind her back. For you, the worker adds. On the house.

The women walk home from the market carrying each other's bouquet; Rebecca with the lilies and tulips, and Charlotte with the daffodils. The storm is drizzling itself out and the ground is wet and ripe. Gray leaves the sky like a wish. I should be happy, Charlotte thinks. Or I should at least feel alive.

Once at Rebecca's apartment building, Charlotte makes a show of placing her bouquet in the bushes outside the entrance, and Rebecca tells her not to be ridiculous, at least leave them in the hallway (the pollen, she's explained, is so dangerous for animals, she doesn't want the flowers inside her apartment even temporarily), but Charlotte likes nuzzling them. Her little secret keeps her feeling powerful until she hides in the bathroom—nausea still acting up from those damn oils, she says—and scrolls to the Rebeccas' wedding photos.

Daffodils.

Smile, Rebecca says when Charlotte reenters the room. A small walk-in closet separates the bathroom from the main room, where the bed and table and love seat are positioned. There isn't room for a couch. Charlotte, fresh off briefly dissociating while washing her hands after pretending to piss, grins widely in the direction of Rebecca's phone but keeps her eyes sad on purpose. Bea greets her by getting off the bed and mouthing her hands. Ordinarily, Charlotte dislikes the warm wet of Bea's tongue, but she is lonely enough to appreciate being acknowledged at all.

Rebecca makes sounds as though she's taking several photos—trying to get good light, or follow the rule of thirds, Charlotte guesses. Rebecca doesn't comment on her expression, hurting Charlotte's feelings, and so she asks what inspired the pictures. Her emotions have dropped into insecure, forlorn—she's got all that fidgety rage up in her belly.

I want to remember you, Rebecca says. Charlotte feels her eyebrows go up. She isn't being broken up with, is she? She can imagine she pales in comparison to Other Rebecca—not because the other Rebecca offers more, but because the Rebeccas seem to share a toxic history. And what is more alluring than a pain you can make fresh whenever you want? Charlotte thinks Rebecca would have loved her and humored her and had a baby with her if they had met first. She asks Rebecca if a palm reader told her she'd be dead soon.

Rebecca laughs. We don't have pictures together, she says. And I don't have any of you.

I send you pictures all the time, Charlotte says, now firmly annoyed. They're forgettable, she adds, sulk already in her voice. I guess? She is thinking: How many selfies? Nudes? At least a few a day, except when she's bloated or sleeping at Liv's. She wonders if Rebecca would be more attentive if Charlotte were tighter with her purse.

I don't see you the way you see yourself, Rebecca says, and Charlotte feels unmoored. A temporary delight warms her; she loves being witnessed, and she especially loves being missed. What image does Rebecca hold of her only she can see? Charlotte fancies herself pretty, but she fantasizes about being beautiful enough to haunt wounded women. Charlotte makes a mental note to discuss the photos with Liv, who has similar issues with the dichotomy of being desired and being missed. (Liv, a secret astrology buff, says this is because of her own Gemini moon.)

And how do you see me, Charlotte asks, her voice meek. Her thought experiments tend to leave her exhausted, as though she's lived whole lives in the minute or two she's spent inside her head. Her self-criticism is back and she's waiting for Rebecca's mean side to finally come out and for her to voice everything she tells herself: self-centered, oblivious, ditzy, weak.

Work with me, Rebecca tells her. I'm waiting for the light.

The women share the small space surprisingly well, Charlotte decides, given all of its history. Rebecca directing and shuffling and Charlotte moving her head one way and then another. Even Bea cooperates for photos, her eyes turning loving when facing her foster mother. The Rebeccas lived in a number of apartments before this one, so Charlotte tries to remind herself it wasn't as though all the good of their relationship sat alongside all the bad. And this was the space the Rebeccas separated in. She told herself those demons had to be the hardest to strip. All *goodbye, goodbye*.

You're really beautiful, Rebecca says finally, and Charlotte's face relaxes, and Rebecca gives a wide smile. Got it, she says.

Let me see. Charlotte closes the space between them quickly, just two or three long steps, and Rebecca locks her phone screen and tosses it onto the bed. She says she needs to tell her something first.

Why first, Charlotte says.

I don't know, Rebecca says. I don't want to lose my nerve.

Charlotte, again, doesn't feel good. She tries to make her face neutral and waits for Rebecca to begin. Rebecca speaks steadily and softly and Charlotte immediately assumes this speech has been workshopped by her sponsor. It's fine, Charlotte tells herself. It's fine. Charlotte sometimes worries she has inherited her father's control issues; does she micromanage and sneak and plan because she wants everyone to be good and happy or because she can only be happy if they seem good and happy? Charlotte loves to quiet a complaint before it's said. Listen, Charlotte tells herself as Rebecca speaks. Stay here.

My wife and I are applying to be foster parents together, she is saying. We'll attend some classes, meet some people . . . I don't know why, she continues quickly, as though sensing Charlotte's impulse to interrupt. But it's really important to me that our application is accepted, so we're going to do our best.

Mm-hmm, Charlotte says. Don't ask her if they're going to raise the baby together, she tells herself. Don't ask again.

We're going in a few days, Rebecca continues. Classes are held in Dupont. Because Charlotte hates herself, she asks if she can meet Rebecca after to pick her up; it would be chaos to do so, of course, and she doesn't want to out herself. And, too, that's exactly what she wants. Charlotte says an iced tea might be nice after sitting in a stuffy old building for that long.

I'm letting you know because it means my wife and I will be seeing each other, Rebecca continues as though Charlotte hadn't said anything. We'll be in touch to coordinate, and I know you don't like it when you feel I'm hiding our contact. Rebecca pauses and appears to reconsider her next sentence. I really respect you, and what we're doing here, and I don't want you to feel misled.

Charlotte feels misled. Though she also knows she is being unreasonable; one doesn't go on sugaring apps for the kind of relationship she keeps pretending she has with Rebecca. Charlotte asks Rebecca if they're breaking up and before Rebecca can answer, she asks why she let her buy her flowers. Before Rebecca can answer that, Charlotte realizes she's been speaking only in her own head, and so she says: Thank you.

Rebecca appears relieved. She hugs Charlotte from behind and holds her phone out in front of Charlotte's face, a rare peek of Rebecca's inner world. The background photo isn't of the Rebeccas (like it was a few weeks into seeing each other, when Charlotte first stole a look: a couple selfie, the two of them laughing in some terribly well-framed candid) but simply black. Replace it, Charlotte was thinking. With me.

Look, Rebecca says. She flips to one of several dozen photos of Charlotte. Charlotte feels disdain. She looks away and Rebecca uses her nose to nudge her head back. I'm so ugly, Charlotte thinks. What do I have to be happy about, she thinks. I'm not loved.

Rebecca whispers, Do you see it? She sounds like a girl with a secret.

Charlotte says no and tries not to cry. Her self-hate is never as magnified as when she is getting what she thought she wanted: herself, alone, memorialized. She keeps thinking: What are we doing what are we doing what are doing what are we doing.

Rebecca clucks and zooms in to the last shot. Charlotte breathes out. The picture hardly caught Charlotte's attention, but now, a stretch of white light she had dismissed as an unfortunate glare from the enormous window above Rebecca's bed clearly has some color in it, some pop, and Charlotte realizes she's seeing something of a rainbow across her torso.

Come on, Rebecca says. What do you see?

I don't know, Charlotte says, because she does, and she is embarrassed.

Tell me, Rebecca says. Please?

A belly, Charlotte says. The half-moon, she adds, pointing at the exaggerated curve big enough for ten babies. She feels loved and stupid, like a child. Rebecca kisses the lonely place behind Charlotte's earlobe and flips her phone to its rear-facing camera.

We look like a home, Rebecca says after she presses the button. Charlotte glances at the screen and sees her eyes are closed. A shard of light swoops out from around them, like an oversized hope. Good, she thinks. Good.

7

IN MY LIVING ROOM, I STRIP. OFF COMES THE white button-down shirt, off comes the black straight-leg pants. My shoes came off at the door, bare feet slick and swollen on the beige rug. I wonder if a forensic anthropologist could retrace my steps, could find evidence of my sweaty footsteps and create a story of my final moments, should I be smacked over the head with a blunt object. With my sports bra stuck around my head, my nose pressed into the wet white cotton, I realize I am giving any intruder the perfect amount of time to slip out the back door with whatever they might want to take. I wonder if intruders would notice our uneven couch and its broken front legs. The stained cushions we do not ask one another questions about because it would ruin our only place to sit aside from our beds and our floors. If an intruder needed to piss, they would likely take to the backyard. I skulk to the kitchen and remind myself to scrub the bottom of my feet; beneath me, dust and, inexplicably, kernels of sand.

Blank ants scurry when I enter the kitchen and I feel relief that I am still a force other creatures recognize as alive. Too shaky to slice and core an apple I smear peanut butter on all sides and pretend it is caramel. These are good memories that soothe me: one set of parents or another taking me to the coastal fair, all Atlantic chill and smug seagulls, and feeding me desserts from stalls. I take my apple to my bedroom, lick and gnaw at it on my bed, and read reviews of the place I'm supposed to meet my next disaster. At this point, I still plan to blow her off. Maybe watch from the corner and see how sad she is, if at all, and decide on the spot. I tell myself that's what people mean when they say follow your gut.

I open another tab and spend a few minutes registering for yet another sleep trial; they pay well—worryingly well—but over the years I've signed up and blown off intake appointments and never committed. I can't conceive of how secure I'd have to feel in Rebecca's ability to keep herself alive in order to actually go off the grid, in a creepy downtown hospital lab. I feel accomplished when I get the automated message confirming my interest in the following month's study and decide maybe I will meet Charlotte. Why waste a good mood?

I sort the reviews by one-star first as a means of managing my expectations. People, I learn, really loathe establishments that bring hipsters to the neighborhood. I read about black bean breakfast tacos, red velvet cake by the slice, milkshakes with banana milk. Lavender in just about every form of coffee. I think: Baby baby baby baby baby baby baby baby. When the apple is a core and I have seeds filling the gaps between my teeth, I open a new browser and search: *WHAT DO SOCIAL WORKERS ASK AT HOME INSPECTION MEETING*.

The questions bring me a comfort I did not expect; the standards are hauntingly low. Lead inspection, fire inspection. State and federal clearances. Because we live in D.C., we have to be at least twenty-one. We need a driver's license though technically we do not need to own a vehicle; a relief, because living in the city on little money, neither of us do. We can even be on public assistance; I remember, distantly, my mother refusing to use food stamps when I was a kid, swearing it would get me taken away. My body tenses up—bad memory, bad body. I read on.

Unless we get an infant, the kid needs its own bedroom, so I screenshot that part of the rules and text it to my wife. She replies within the minute and tells me she knows, she's looking at new places; the social worker just comes back if you move. And anyway, she wants a *baby* baby. I can tell she's not going to accept any hints to wait, and I hope this means she's eager for me to move back in. And I think: New home on what money? I can't imagine her stipend increase is enough to afford a bigger place on her own.

Timing wise, the process feels more flexible than her pressure suggests. There's an info session potential parents have to attend, held every Monday and Wednesday morning, some photocopies of IDs and fingerprints. Ten classes called pre-service trainings that, at a glance, appear to cover child development, working with the agency, and emotional regulation. We have a few months to complete those before we need to start the trainings from scratch. Single people can foster as well as couples, and I wonder how soon the agency will notice Rebecca's shifted from married to single after our divorce. I wonder if my wife learned from some online forum of aspiring foster parents that she needed me around. I'm not sure if it's good to be needed but I enjoy the sensation.

On average, I learn, still naked and letting sweat meld with my unmade bed, it takes about five months to get licensed and get a kid. I keep thinking like that: Get a kid. I wonder if my foster family thought of me in such blunt terms when they met me, an event I don't remember but must have happened at least once before I arrived at their home with my trash bag full of stuff. Maybe we went for ice cream. Maybe they weren't allowed to take me from the building and we sat on the floor and played board games. Those sorts of bonding experiences blur with the ones I experienced with my actual parents as they lived between homeless shelters and halfway houses in those years. Teachers, aides, and psychologists mixed in with people I was supposed to understand as family. I understood myself only, and continue to miss that sense of self. Never again have I been allowed to be as angry as I want.

I wonder if my wife and I would play house for one month, in the time between getting a child placement and our divorce eligibility. One month of bliss, comfort, routine. One month of brushing our teeth beside one another. Of holding hands in bed. The third human in the home doesn't enter my imagination, further proof that this is a horrible idea. I transition myself from this fantasy by imagining my wife asking me if I've boiled water for tea and when I say yes, telling me she's printed the divorce papers. I imagine saying no, I haven't yet, but I will, of course I will, and her saying the same. The certainty of an end as something to work toward.

A notification from Charlotte interrupts my reading. Charlotte describes what she is wearing in detail, noting that she asked for my input but when I didn't reply, realized she did not want to be a bother this early into our relationship.

At the word *relationship*, I give my phone a look as if to say, That was fast! Still I read on. She describes herself in a white tank top and beige leggings with white sneakers. She name-drops the sneakers which I immediately google and learn retailed for close to three hundred dollars. My first thought: She's done this before. My second thought: That's a few days of work before taxes. A grand hope: Maybe her parents are loaded. My final thought: If she replies in less than one minute, it's Heads. Longer, Tails.

Immediately: I realized I haven't seen your picture.

I know, I write back. I never respond that quickly, and yet I must play by my own rules: Heads is Heads.

Black T-shirt, I tell her. Miserable aura. Then I turn off my phone.

Thirty minutes turns out to be plenty of time to open my college-era laptop and check my bank account. I have sixteen dollars to last five days, which is more than I expected. One credit card is maxed and closed, so I pay the minimum twenty-four dollars a month. Rent deducts from my checking account, and I'm lucky enough for it to include my share of internet and utilities. Food is meager. I've been swiping tampons and toilet paper from the break room.

The café's menu suggests that if neither of us order food and I pay at the counter and get away with a dollar tip, we'll be fine. I hope Charlotte is the sort of woman who worries eating will make her look like a pig. I feel guilty at my own thoughts and walk faster. I want to tell Charlotte to eat, eat. I want to bring her inside a 7-Eleven and feed her cheese curls and slushies in the parking lot. What place offers more clarity than one under fluorescent lights. I think Charlotte might be flattered if I arrive early, body riveted at the door, disinterested smile in my eyes. What more can women want.

Around me, houses owned by people comfortable in generational wealth. Obvious, of course, by the decidedly unkempt lawns, kitschy welcome mats, and pastel paints on shingles. On my walks to work I sometimes imagine crawling into the ground-floor windows of these houses just to stand. Not to eat the food or watch the television or vomit beneath anyone's pillow. Only to stand. How easy to pretend you belong in a place once your body is present.

Flyers decorate street poles. A few missing pets; I keep my eyes on the bushes, just in case. I would let a small creature nurse from my nipples if it helped. I feel out of control—what am I doing, where is my wife, does she still think of herself as my wife—so I play my game. Heads for drivers I think are abiding the speed limit and Tails for ones that zoom or dawdle. Tails means I'll be normal and Heads means I'll be myself. There, I think. Good.

The other signs are laminated and encourage people to call and email in opposition to a homeless shelter coming to the neighborhood. If I read the details correctly, it seems the shelter would actually be a few blocks from any houses, in a mostly forgotten stretch of city where high schoolers go to smoke. Only one sign mentions it's a shelter for women and children. When I pass a woman pushing a stroller of two I wonder how she feels about the shelter, if she's called or emailed, hung a sign herself. I glance behind myself and see she's squinting at me, hand at forehead, and I hope she's checking me out. I walk until I hear a car coming at just the right speed.

I walk walk walk walk walk walk right into the street, head down, eyes half closed, feet damp as dirt, and when I feel a warm weight collide with my side, I worry not about finding Charlotte but about an ugly and unhappy baby waiting for me. I think: Oh. I think: I do want to be alive.

8

CHARLOTTE CABS TO THE CAFÉ AND THINKS about herself the entire way. She's watching clips of her favorite movie, the 1979 TV special *Jack Frost*, a stop-motion animated masterpiece narrated by Pardon-Me-Pete, a groundhog who is buddies with little old Jack Frost. Her decisions feel out of control, exciting, and too she is nine years old, alone on the couch in the living room, watching the cartoons her parents loved as children while they threatened to divorce in the other room. *Rudolph's Shiny New Year*, *The Year Without a Santa Claus*, *Rudolph and Frosty's Christmas in July*. Weirdo, simplistic, amateur. *Weird.*

The sun is hot and thick and Charlotte thinks she must be really sad, must be really troubled, to cry in the back seat of a car when there's no clouds in the sky. The snow on her small screen regulates her into a socially acceptable numbness. She opens her texts and writes a long one addressed to herself to, as Rebecca put it, process her feelings.

Does she want her to relapse? No. That would be cruel, she reasons. Abusive. Charlotte quickly concludes she merely wants Rebecca to go against herself—shout and push and threaten and run away and run right back—so Charlotte is sure she isn't the biggest sucker in the world, helping her to get a baby when she's not even divorced yet. Charlotte types and deletes the truer and scarier realization: Charlotte doesn't trust love that doesn't feel earned. She sends her Rebecca a few e-gift cards for coffee and groceries, hoping for a confirmation of receipt, if not a full conversation.

The driver asks if she needs him to call someone and she tells him no, no, she's fine, really. Charlotte keeps her hand on her belly. He asks if it's her husband giving her trouble. No, Charlotte says, smiling. She's the sort of femme who appreciates the humor of her secrets. They are quiet until he has to make a U-turn to pull her up right to the curb. They really need to put stoplights here, he tells her. She feels certain she's never been treated so delicately, though she has, of course, been doted upon nearly all her life.

The café is a buttercup cream and Charlotte feels worse. She really wants to discuss her status with Rebecca and she also wants to show up at Rebecca's apartment, which feels unwise. She thinks. There are other pregnant people around, fascinating and upsetting her with their visibility. Without her bump, Charlotte can be clueless and ask a million questions, stare and ogle; with it, she is wary of people she suspects even marginally of being pregnant. Other pregnant people are uniquely positioned to comment on how far along she appears to be. She's never been called out directly, but she leaves all such encounters with the terrible, shameful feeling that every single one of them knows. There she goes, transparent as dust bunny webs.

Liv, Charlotte texts, elbows on the table. I'm gonna send you some $$ for you to get a calzone from the hot food bar . . .

You don't need to do that!!!

I already sent it hehe

Are you coming by?? What am i getting for you

There's a good table in the corner, i've had my eye on it since yesterday LOL

I'm in the studio . . .

I'll drop it by for you

There it is. Charlotte relaxes. She doesn't like being manipulative but she doesn't entirely know how to get what she wants, which at the moment is for Olivia to pick up a bird-of-paradise, leave it at Rebecca's apartment as a little surprise, and then, sure, eat the calzone from the hot food bar with the good red peppers. Maybe she'll even end up in Rebecca's line. A free agent who can report back without seeming suspicious. All the figures can stay in place, happy for a while.

She wants to leave her Rebecca and be chased. Not forever. Not even for a terribly long time; just around the block once or twice, maybe onto a crowded bus or into the lobby of a fashionably old hotel. A little drama, a little skin in the game. How else can she feel certain she is not a joke? She decides she has little to lose.

Somewhere in the café, a baby fusses and Charlotte pivots away, embarrassed for whoever is responsible for the little hellion. The walls are glass. Charlotte keeps her hands on her belly and watches people enter and leave the little establishment; at least two older women give her a look of knowing, and though Charlotte is not attracted to either of them, she wants them to strip her naked and compliment her lack of stretch marks. A woman who has time to moisturize is a woman who will have plenty of time to stare at her baby. Charlotte rubs her belly and rubs her belly and rubs her belly. She wonders if her date will want to go down on her and if she'll be smooth enough to play coy and keep her top on to conceal her bump.

The fussing people sit next to Charlotte. The original fusser keeps dropping their binky and the women keep picking it up off the ground and returning it to the baby's mouth. This feels odd to Charlotte but also good. She gets looks sometimes, bumping into stuff with her stomach, jogging across the street without cradling her belly with both hands. Little tells, little giveaways that things aren't what they seem. But people treat real babies badly all the time. Except Charlotte. Charlotte, Charlotte thinks, is so nice.

Hi, she says once, then a second time. She is fishing for a pack of baby wipes in her tote; she keeps them on hand because her mother has a phobia of public bathroom toilet paper, convinced it's all been sprayed with disease, and also because Olivia prefers them when she's having stomach issues after eating her daily meal. The women, she realizes, are watching her. Their smiles are wide and not friendly.

If you need them, Charlotte continues. Sometimes she loves being stared at, watched with her belly on; she's the spinning dancer in the snow globe, the safest, prettiest girl in the world. No one reaches for the wipes.

You're so sweet, a woman not holding the baby says.

Totally, another woman adds. But we are all set.

Charlotte nods, says, Oh okay I was just wondering, and the women nod back, clearly irritated by her ongoing intrusion, and the person holding the baby still hasn't said a word, and Charlotte is feeling very small and stupid, and then the binky is rolling on the floor again. The women stand up. Charlotte rises after the women, slowly, holding her stomach, wipes still in her hands. Charlotte watches the woman's lackeys squat down and search on her behalf.

Charlotte asks, Sisters, and the woman says, Lesbians, actually, loudly, and Charlotte says, Oh, me too, and the woman says over her screaming baby that Charlotte is a liar and she says, Hmm, because she must have misheard it and the lackeys are moving chair legs around, looking and looking, and Charlotte stays standing, belly out, feet on the floor.

The woman holding the baby holds her hand out—to Charlotte, to anyone. Pacifier, she says. Please. Her voice is singsong, like she's asking a spoiled child for the return of a stolen toy. Charlotte smiles. So weird, she says. Must have gone the other way.

It's really not under there, she asks. Her voice creaks, like it has not often been used at this particular register. It occurs to Charlotte that she and the woman might both be having breakdowns.

Nope, Charlotte says. Don't see a thing.

The women search, and the baby fusses, and Olivia calls and calls and calls. Charlotte doesn't move her feet, presses down so hard her sneakers have that silicone flat against the floor, and Charlotte almost doesn't hear it when the woman says *I know*. It's impressive, how quick and quiet the baby holder is, with all her meanness and rightness.

When the women are out the door, Charlotte cries loudly and efficiently in the café. No one moves away from her, but she can tell they're considering it. She figures the people typing on their computers are hoping the tears end when the call does. They probably think some guy is blowing her off again. Or that her father is going in for an emergency heart surgery.

Charlotte tells Olivia she's so, so sorry, she's ashamed of herself, she needs help. She wants to talk about intentionally going into Rebecca's first wife's line at the market, how it felt really weird and really good. How she can't stop pushing Rebecca, how she can't play second fiddle to what feels like Rebecca's real life—sobriety, walking her dog, finishing her degree. Being good and patient and wifely. So why can't Charlotte let the belly go? She wants to map every minute detail of her life, so Olivia can pinpoint the roots of her self-sabotage. She's talking about her pain so intensely Olivia speaks over her and tells her not to cry, love, you'll ruin your face, and Charlotte gets just a little louder, and when she feels a big burp coming up, she tries to mold it into a gasp. She fails and her chest hurts. She hangs up.

For you, a worker mouths from the other side of her table. Charlotte notices they've left some napkins. She wipes her eyes, though she can still see okay, and looks to the window. She has at least a few minutes until the new woman should arrive, but she doesn't know how ruffled she wants to appear.

Olivia calls back. Charlotte holds her belly with one hand and reminds both herself and Olivia that pregnancy hormones are wild, aren't they? Olivia reminds Charlotte she is worried, and also that she used Charlotte's saved credit card for the calzone. Charlotte reminds Olivia about the pending plant purchase. Olivia scoffs and tells her to get off that shit and then honking from the street interrupts Charlotte's attention. She swears she can hear birds through the glass windows of the restaurant telling her to *hurry up, hurry up, life is changing.*

Holy shit, Charlotte says. I have to go.

You're meeting someone?

No, Charlotte says, but she's thinking, Yes, she's thinking, It's got that fated feeling, she's thinking, Can I be so chosen. To Olivia, she adds: I think I just saw someone get hit by a car? Olivia asks how that can be a question—did they get hit or didn't they—and Charlotte answers by hanging up, bouncing the binky into her purse, and bolting for the door. She and her baby do, after all, enjoy a little limelight.

9

THE DRIVER CALLS ME A FUCKFACE. I DON'T HAVE insurance, she says. What the hell are you thinking? I was thinking Heads but when the word leaves my mouth her face stays the same, mad and confused. I'm still sitting on the street, watching her second-guess what happened. Had she been texting? Thinking about an ex? Or was it really the pedestrian's fault, being careless, playing games, stepping into the street on a dare and then stumbling into the car?

I didn't hit you, she says. You, like, collided with my car.

Okay, I say. I'm enjoying the adrenaline so much that I consider bailing on my date; I'm a person, I guess, or I wouldn't have a heart to race.

It's different, the driver says. I realize she has her blinker on.

You can go, I say. It doesn't matter.

Cool, she says. She doesn't hesitate. I miss the driver until a pregnant lady sits beside me. I listen closely and realize she's crying a little. Not hysterical, but I'll take it.

I almost lost you, she says. Before I had you.

You're okay, I tell her, and I wonder if she shouldn't be the one reassuring me. Did we both get hit? She's hot, so I decide the explanation for her emotions comes down to hormones. She doesn't care about your life, I tell myself. She just doesn't want to witness something fucked-up and transfer the bad vibes to her baby.

We're okay, she says. She's still crying. I ask her if she needs a hug and she scoots right into me. A ride share pulls up a few inches from our feet and I tell the driver to fucking watch himself. He keeps his window up but I feel the woman purr her approval into me. I wonder if Charlotte is here watching from a café window.

We're okay, I repeat. I wonder if I can get this woman to lift her dress; I bet she's wearing biker shorts to cover her underwear in case of a breeze, and I'm aroused at the thought of putting my nose to her crotch and finding a wet spot.

You might have a concussion, she says. We should go to the hospital.

No, I tell her. Not a chance. I blurt that I don't have insurance.

Urgent care, she says. Is there anyone I can call?

I pull out my phone. No new messages—including from Charlotte. I wonder if she's bailed and tell myself to make decisions that make my life easier; if she's disappeared, let her go. Tails: Let it go. Belly repeats herself, asking louder and slower if she can help me call anyone, and I shake my head gingerly. My wife is the person I should call, but I don't want to worry her. I refuse to see a doctor or a nurse or anyone who has any expectation of being paid for their time. I tell myself to look up what to do after you've been hit by a car when I get back to my room; someone else without insurance must have vlogged it.

No one, I say, and my vulnerability surprises me. What about you, I say, eager to take the attention off me. You good?

I'm worried about you, she says. I'm responsible.

Why would you be responsible, I tell her. You aren't the driver. Right? I wonder if maybe I am a little fucked-up. I look around and try to spot the car I walked into and realize I can't remember its color, much less its make or model. I imagine the driver crawling out her window after hitting me and then dragging my injured self into her trunk. No one would find me.

Right, I repeat, louder, and she jumps a little and holds her belly.

You're so confused, she says. It's okay. I saw it happen from inside, I'd been waiting . . .

For the arches of Heaven, I fill in. Or the gates of hell?

She flinches then looks pleased, delighted, even, then says no, she's waiting for a woman from an app. Her eyes have that eager look I recognize in fellow femme women; look at us, dyking out in plain sight. I sense she's waiting for me to ask if she's making friends or waiting for a date and so instead I tell her I've got to get going, I'm meeting someone too.

Thanks, I tell her, though she didn't do much of anything except confuse me more. Charlotte still hasn't texted, and I'm moody, deflated. My body already hurts.

She takes my hands and doesn't let them go.

Where do you live, she says.

D.C., I say, and she rolls her eyes. I name the street my wife lives on and she nods. She asks if I know the date and I pretend to think and then get it wrong by a day. She asks my birthday and I give her the real one because she might be one of those astrology queers and it'll be a headache to change it later. When she asks my name, I almost don't tell her; something about her stare, the lack of blinking, excites me, makes me feel haunted. Where is Charlotte, I'm thinking. Where is that little flake?

You're here to meet Charlotte, she says, as though she's a hostess confirming a reservation. I don't look around. I don't look at my phone. I didn't even ask for her ID. I'm a good girl; I nod. I let her keep holding my hands. No, I embrace hers back. I'm active. A participant.

When I bring Charlotte—Charlotte, Charlotte, Charlotte—inside, it occurs to me that an insurance payout might have been nice, but being desired is nicer. We're sitting down while Charlotte looks up local urgent care clinics. I can walk you, she says. Or get us a car. She names the popular apps, then takes them back, saying those companies are horrible to drivers. A yellow cab, she says. What do you think about that?

Just coffee, I tell her. And you. I pause and look at her middle. Do they have a good decaf here, I ask. Or are you okay to have regular? I really can't remember if caffeine restrictions during pregnancy are based on science or societal shaming. I add a wink, feeling ridiculous. Being smooth about the pregnancy feels necessary; I can't quite believe I skimmed that detail in her profile or that I would have forgotten it.

When she beams, it's a different kind of orgasm. I'm thinking about the side of my body, the hip I think hit the car. I'm afraid to step into the bathroom to look. I plan to root through her wallet while she's pissing, take what I can, and I push that away because it's not the energy I wanted to bring into this meeting. I wonder if we might have sex and if it's assumed that I would service or if she's hoping I'll be charmed if she gives it her best shot. Just the idea gives me anxiety.

I'm going to get a green tea, she says. I'm allowed a little caffeine. She asks if I'm in pain and I tell her I'm too embarrassed.

Now *that* I understand, Charlotte says. We're good at protecting ourselves. I tell her I agree, that I *feel seen.*

You didn't include a recent picture, I tell her, because I want to stay in control and I can't stop thinking about it. I feel guilty around the kids in the store, like my bad character is more easily visible to them. I wouldn't have agreed to this meetup if I thought I'd have to pay for someone's baby. I almost say that I'd just be with my wife if I was going to do that. Instead my brain inserts her face over Charlotte's and I have to pinch my inner wrists to keep from throwing up. Charlotte doesn't reply right away, but reddens, so I tell her I'm disappointed. By what, I don't know. What I do know is I want to see how much hurt she'll take.

Before I walked into traffic, I was on a forum for sugar parents. I did not love the use of such a normie word as *parent* but I was immediately unsettled by the color schemes of forums for sugar daddies. I could not find anything specific to lesbian sugaring that did not come with a warning about possible phishing schemes.

People are targeted, she says. Like, for their babies. She mimes as though someone is cutting an enormous hole around the outside of her stomach. I'm just trying to be really cautious, she tells me. With what I share about myself.

Shit, I say. Just like that, I'm myself again.

It's okay, she says softly. I should have told you. She blinks across the table at me and I blink back feeling stupid and she tells me she is ravenous. I tell her I would never want to keep a pregnant person hungry while I'm thinking: Oh fuck me, I can't afford hungry. Our table is a small circle. Too small for me to pretend not to hear her. I ask her if she tends to cook at home or not and she tells me she has a meal kit mailed to her every week.

You know, she says. Everything is chopped and portioned for you, and you just put it on the stove. I tell her I know what meal kits are, though I leave out that I am only familiar with them because we sell custom kits at the market. They retail for one hundred dollars per person, per week. Lo-fi pop surrounds us and I notice gravel in both of my palms. I don't remove it.

Charlotte reads the menu out loud, further embarrassing me. She reads descriptions for blueberry vanilla cupcakes, lemon custard pie, chia pudding with raspberries, chia pudding with hazelnut cacao, chia pudding supreme. She rubs her belly with one hand the entire time she speaks. I interrupt her and ask what *supreme* refers to and she just giggles, shrugs, tells me there's no explanation. I can look at the menu in front of me but I don't. I want her to feel useful and I want to give myself time to think.

I order a black coffee and iced water. The waiter asks if I'd like lemon or lime and, to be funny, I say, Both, but neither of the people listening to me laugh. I'm humiliated and small-feeling so I come up with a Heads or Tails: Heads, I'm a good girl, and Tails, I make a scene. Heads if he smiles with his eyes, Tails if he doesn't.

The waiter types my request into his iPad, eyebrows straight and level, as though he is worried I won't tip if he messes up. There's a smile but he's eye-dead. I resent his effort because I know an emotional connection makes it all the harder to slip out while the bill prints. I tell myself to think harder, to leave fewer stains.

Charlotte orders us two slices of cake. One white with cherry frosting and one blueberry with lemon curd. The slices alone top the sixteen dollars in my account. To share, she tells me, perhaps noticing my hesitation. When the waiter walks away, I tell her I wasn't expecting to eat so much sugar. She drops her face as though I've slapped her. I can't blame her—I am not a good person. I add that I only worry about the pregnancy.

Or is that not true, I continue slowly, as though I hadn't just hurt her feelings. Is a binge during pregnancy fine and people are just being fatphobic about it?

No, she says equally slowly. That is true, about monitoring sugar. Her eyes are big wet holes and I accept I've hurt her enough to hate myself; I've gotten too cold, too dry, and Charlotte doesn't want my cruelty. Charlotte doesn't even want me, just my money to take care of her baby. My inability to provide for her at all is what I feel worst about.

You can take some home, she adds. A damp towel will keep the frosting from drying out. Her face communicates she is regretting her vulnerability, wishing she wasn't the sort of woman who met up with women like me. She looks around and sees, I guess, all the pairs of two in the room. She likely assumes they are happy, splitting their well-sculpted deserts.

Nothing would make me happier, I tell her, than to feed you sweets.

This café is more ideal for a second date, as it fosters a sort of closeness Charlotte and I do not yet have. With her face turned away from mine, I feel safe enough to really look at her. I see she did a poor job of contouring the sides of her nose, a detail most people would not notice, but I know where to look to find people as insecure as myself. I decide I would like to kiss her nostrils. I tell her as much and she laughs. Just before the cake arrives, she taps my knuckles with a smirk. If dirt is transferred from my hands to hers, she doesn't tell me.

The slices are impressive in size and in design.

Frosting on the top and between three layers but not on the sides, an aesthetic choice that only works when words like *organic*, *natural*, and *fuel* appear on the menu. Charlotte takes out her phone and tugs the plates toward her for a photo. Or for many photos. I lean out of frame as a courtesy. My wife has run a small-scale food blog since before we started dating, and over the years I have learned about natural light and prime angles. I offered my hands again and again, to hold a plate, to hold a knife, to pour syrup into the center of a pancake, but in one of her most loving moments, she told me my fingers were not aesthetic. It's weird, she'd said straight to my face. You're so skinny but your fingers are like sausages. I limit myself to three social media checks a week from a burner account. Across from Charlotte, I put my hands in my lap and ask what got her into food photography.

I like angles, she says. Tricks with light.

How do you fill your time, I say. Looking for light? The conversation feels off-kilter, fun. I'm thinking of when I was dating my wife. Her reluctance to tell me increases my curiosity.

So you're the weirdo, I say in her silence. You're my weirdo. I feel she's performing, tap-dancing through the dullest daydreams. So nervous, so dodgy like a bird, I want to lick her skin to the bone.

I'm unique, she says in a way that convinces me she doesn't entirely love herself. I let that vulnerability sit— I'd give the world to know what to do, what to say—and Charlotte tells me she's an artist.

Lots of spiders, she adds. Clay and paint.

That's your work, I say, trying to tone down my delight. That's your day? I'm trying to figure out how to ask her where this baby came from but I know I'm not supposed to do that. To appear friendlier, I lean forward in my seat. I wish she would go to the bathroom so I could peek inside her wallet and make sure she brought her own credit card or cash.

Eye contact is still a struggle and I wonder if she thinks my apparent disinterest is sexy or frustrating or both. I wonder what healthy food looks like to Charlotte and imagine us eating those fifteen-dollar salads in a park. She is probably the kind of woman who orders extras of the luscious parts, the avocado and feta and salmon. I cannot remember the last time I comfortably ordered an item that was not the cheapest option on a menu. Months into dating, my wife assumed I was a vegetarian as I never ordered meat for precisely that reason. When is a lie not more comfortable than a truth? When it's time to swallow, I thank Charlotte for feeding me. She gives a full-mouth smile that suggests she still wears her retainer at night. Somehow, she has avoided getting frosting stuck to her teeth.

I encourage Charlotte to tell me more about what her days look like and she does. She alludes to hours spent at a studio, though I can't tell if she's referring to someone's apartment or a place where people make art. Spin with Olivia, who I guess is an ex-girlfriend, and half hours spent reading in public parks. She makes a point of working from a local coffee shop at least once a week while her cleaning person comes.

I feel bad being in there while she's working, she explains. It's like, how could I not get in the way? So I leave and Venmo her when she's done.

I ask if the worker ever does a poor job and Charlotte says no, not really. She adds she isn't allowed to dust the spiders.

No dusting the spiders, I repeat. Does she dance with them instead? Charlotte looks startled, and I wonder if I've offended her. Then she laughs and tells me we should do it ourselves sometime, break our legs in a little old web.

If we could end this scene, she says, smirking, we'd have such good smiles for the audience at home. I clap my hands between our faces like a director's clapboard and a baby yelps from somewhere in the room. Charlotte winks at me.

To keep myself feeling powerful, I imagine knocking the table into Charlotte's lap and feel relief at my big solution. I feel I am a little smart, a little proactive, a little strategic. I sip my coffee and make sure it is not terribly hot. I want to drink all of it but tell myself I am holding back for the greater good. When the waiter reappears to offer a refill, I'm thinking: Tails. I stick my foot out and, making me as happy as can be, he slips forward and the coffee slathers the table. Actually, no. It slathers mostly me.

Later, when I nurse my swollen skin at home, alone in my bedroom, I tell myself I am smart, I am not bad, I am just fine. I am not noble and I am not the worst I could be. I am not going to sue the place, of course. I am not going to leave a bad review on the internet. I accepted the comped bill, made a show of tipping a few dollars anyway, encouraged Charlotte to bring home the leftover cake. She gave me a look that said she had hoped I would offer. What a delight to meet her expectations before the stakes mattered. I even told Charlotte to call me by my full name, a choice that felt dangerous in its reminders of my wife. Rebecca, she said. She spoke like she said it all the time, like her mouth was a well-rehearsed dancer. Rebecca.

Charlotte

10

CHARLOTTE AND OLIVIA MET OUTSIDE THE REN-
wick Gallery on Pennsylvania Ave. just after eleven. The
girls think of the museum as their darling. It should be
tourist central considering it was the first museum in
the nation, not to mention how close it is to the White
House, but it's much smaller than other Smithsonians in
the area and people aren't always charmed by the adver-
tised arts and crafts focus of the space.

I can't believe it, Olivia says. She looks genuinely dis-
tressed at the crowded entrance.

What did you have for breakfast, Charlotte says. She's
feeling shaken from her date with Other Rebecca, as well
as her Rebecca's hard boundary on her belly. Charlotte
is hoping today's exhibit, Frances Glessner Lee's *Nutshell*
crime dollhouses, will help clear her head.

Do you think these people are part of a class field trip, Olivia continues.

The exhibit is really popular, Charlotte says. Let's eat and come back. Charlotte feels they're being surrounded on all sides, by tourists with their big backpacks and red baseball caps. Seeing people excited about art gets Charlotte feeling embarrassed, hopeful; maybe people do still like to look at weird stuff and think about it.

I want to see the exhibit, Olivia says. We're already here.

Let's get your appetite up, Charlotte says. These people will be gone when we're back.

THE LADIES PASS the vape back and forth on the walk to the food truck. They share two lunch specials with hummus and pita and olives and fries with za'atar. There are chopped cucumbers and tomatoes in a lemon, mint, and olive oil dressing. They drink water from glass bottles and Olivia prompts Charlotte to sit in the sun; Olivia's wrists in the picture make Charlotte feel unhappy and nauseated. She puts food into her mouth while strangers walk by. She wonders how many webs are in the legs of the bench.

This is a great reset, Olivia says. You're the best.

Charlotte covers her falafel with hot sauce and asks if Olivia noticed any ranch dressing anywhere.

Sorry, she says. The communal ranch is no longer available at this location. Olivia pauses in scooping hummus up with her fingers and looks beneath the bench. I hope the rats are enjoying their spoils.

The museum is at capacity and the girls join the line. Charlotte regrets not wearing her belly. She's trying to give Olivia a good day to brighten her spirits and the belly is an immediate downer; Olivia wouldn't be complaining if they got a little special access right now.

Is it all people taking pictures, Olivia says, kicking up on her tiptoes. Did someone famous come here?

Artists, Charlotte says, feeling dread. No one likes to pontificate like artists.

Meetup groups, the man doing a bag check at the door says.

True crime folks, another guard says. Mommy and Me groups.

We're in all these pictures, Olivia says once the girls enter the exhibit. It's unavoidable.

Charlotte surveys the room. The exhibit is made up of eighteen dioramas all made by Lee, a forensic scientist. The pieces are permanently housed at the Office of the Chief Medical Examiner in Baltimore, where police still use them as training tools. Charlotte curses herself for not being more proactive in coming to the exhibit before it became a thing; if she were a cooler, smarter, more efficient person, she'd have already documented all the precious details. Now people are hustling from piece to piece, taking pictures and talking about figuring it all out later. Slow down, Charlotte thinks. Be here. She understands she should take her own advice, but she can't yet see what she's doing.

Ignore them, Charlotte says. Just help me get a good spot.

The dioramas are in glass boxes around the room. Against the walls and in rows through the middle. Charlotte feels warm and overwhelmed. What am I doing thinking my art has a place in this world, Charlotte thinks as someone lowers their phone and huffs as she interrupts their shot. Who am I to think the public would adore me?

Do you think people would be interested in micro oils, Olivia says. Tiny paintings on tiny walls . . . tiny coffee-table books with tiny covers . . .

You're so entrepreneurial, Charlotte says. It's your business degree.

I need to survive, Olivia says. We're not all you.

I'm wasting their help, Charlotte says. I'm using all their love up. Charlotte feels elbows all around her. She wonders how many of the guards know CPR.

You can sell your stuff so easily, Olivia says. Do you have any idea how much people charge for their key chains online? Polymer stuff is in.

I don't want to sell key chains, Charlotte says. The people behind her are taking pictures over her shoulder— she watches them zoom in on the screens, avoiding her completely. She stares into the glass and hopes her reflection makes it in every shot.

Ashtrays, Olivia continues. Jewelry dishes. Ring holders . . . just think about the spider legs—

I've tried this, Charlotte says. Liv, we've tried this. The Instagram shop? All those pop-up markets I messaged? It just doesn't feel right.

Nothing feels right for anyone, she says. Selling art sucks.

I don't have enough to sell. If enough orders came in I'd just end up behind—

It might give you a sense of purpose, Olivia says. A project outside your . . . romantic endeavors.

Hurry, Charlotte says, yanking them into an open spot. They're looking into an apartment where a woman lies on the living room floor. She's got a pie in the oven, she's got canned food in the kitchen. Magazines with covers. What condition is the bed in? Are there stains on the floor—where's that splatter? The level of detail is astronomical; you can check the lock, there's no sign of a forced entry. There are rugs up against the door . . . are we looking at a suicide instead of a home invasion? It's no secret that solving these dioramas is not the point; there's no right answer, especially not if you're thinking in terms of making an arrest. The dioramas are exercises in detail, both for the creator and the observer.

Your own little world, Olivia says. Your empire.

I want only the willing, Charlotte says. She's seeing her Rebeccas made of pink clay, five inches tall, heads round like baby bellies. The frame freezes and the Rebeccas are slashed without weapons—they bear identical wounds, their heads and arms and legs sliced with air. Bea, a short red pony, gloms over to eat them.

Yeah, Olivia says. You can call it Charlotte's Web.

Do you try to be repulsive, she says.

Olivia gives her a look. Do you? Charlotte's saved by Rebecca calling.

I feel like we barely scratched the surface, Charlotte says instead of hello. Can we know each other more?

I don't think you've earned that yet, Other Rebecca says after a pause. She asks Charlotte if she's familiar with Kalorama. It's the neighborhood Charlotte spent much of her youth in, waltzing in and out of friends' old money homes. It's where at least one former president lives.

I've been around, she says. Sure. She's wondering why in the hell her Rebecca is saving her pennies if her wife has access to this kind of wealth, but this Rebecca says she's watching a friend's place while they're out of town, and maybe she'll invite her over sometime.

There's oat-based gelato outside, Olivia says, looking at her phone. It's a pop-up truck.

There's a pool, Rebecca adds, and Charlotte can't help but be impressed. Private pools are rare in the city and it is so damn hot. She's wondering why her Rebecca didn't house-sit for this friend to make money or just sit in a bigger space. Charlotte envisions herself perched naked on the end of a diving board, both Rebeccas fretting from the water below.

Maybe we can cool you off, real Rebecca says. I can't imagine how hard it is to be pregnant right now.

Right, Charlotte says, hands stilling on her flat belly. I'd love to get wet with you. Inside she is thinking fuck fuck fuck. Can she pull off a one-piece without seams showing? She blurts that she actually feels a little better covered, what with her body *changing* and all, and the other Rebecca sounds serious, concerned.

I'm really glad you told me that, she says. She doesn't lower her voice into any kind of a whisper, just tells Charlotte she'll let her keep her top on so long as she's fine with her breasts being pulled up and out. Charlotte makes a noise like Huh and Oh.

This is nauseating, Olivia whispers loudly. You're disturbing the peace.

Perfect, Charlotte says. She's feeling bashful, gauche; the attentiveness feels good, giggly.

You haven't told me the name, she says.

I don't know, Charlotte says.

The other Rebecca laughs from what sounds like a deep place. Charlotte doesn't ask why, just waits until it's time to say goodbye.

When Charlotte is off the phone, Olivia doesn't have any quips. She seems subdued, tired. Charlotte has a funny vision, Olivia rolling her eyes in a thin hospital bed. The air chops her up and when Charlotte catches her head, she's too eager, too excited—her thick fingers go right through her eyes, dream-Olivia's whole head just clay. Put that thought away, Charlotte thinks. Close that whole house up and board the windows.

11

AT MY REGISTER, I'M ALL ITCH. MY SKIN FLAKES beneath my nails and when I bite my fingers, I marvel at my own taste. There is something special in experiencing yourself. Minus nannies and interns running errands for rich bosses, the store is dead. I sense the manager is close to walking the floor and sending people home early so I watch my posture and tell myself to look alive. This manager is among my least favorite, as she has an unfortunate habit of pointing out my unhappiness. You look drowsy, she tells me some mornings. Remember to smile at customers, she adds when I scan out her protein packs. If we made a commission I might smile more but we don't and so I don't. When she passes me, I give her a thumbs-up. She looks at me and through me, easy, as if I were a ghost or a myth.

I think about what I would do with two unscheduled

hours. I think I would walk two blocks to the middle school and watch kids play softball. That sounds slimy—I don't trust adults who spend too much time looking at kids—but what I want to see is how parents pass off juice boxes, Capri-Suns, peanut butter and jelly sandwiches without the crust. Do the mothers smile the whole time, or only when the child is approaching? I imagine the mothers and nannies and big sisters and little sisters and aunts and grandmothers frown the whole time. Kids, I think, get peanut butter on their fingers. Lick it off their own chins with frowns. Sneeze into open palms and keep eating with frowns. If I were a mother, I like to think I would lick my kid's palms, spit and snot and jelly smears and all, and when my tongue was back in my mouth, the kid and I would give each other the nod. When a real mother stands in front of me and snaps her fingers, I tell her to eat shit.

She says, Excuse me? There's a baby looking up at me from its stroller. The little face is all, Wow. The woman looks ready to knock her fist straight up my nose. She repeats her question in a way that lets me know she heard exactly what I said.

I say, Um. I tell her I'm sorry, I was just speaking under my breath. It's a habit, I say, talking to myself when it's slow. I know she looks familiar but I can't place it.

You tell yourself such dirty things, she says. You really do? Her willingness to stay in her anger amazes me. I wonder if she's ever let a woman go down on her. I tell her I am not sure, I don't think about it, but I guess so. I tell her I didn't realize she was standing there. I nod at the kid and tell her I wouldn't swear in front of a child. As soon as it's out of my mouth, I think, Would I? I probably would.

You don't care about my kid, the woman says. You don't care about shit.

I shrug. I look toward the end of my register where my bagger usually stands and, of course, no one is there. Too dead to have people waiting to fold bags, and besides, she's already on her way out of town with that girlfriend. Camping in Shenandoah, I think, though it might be a memory or a lie I made up to fill in a gap of my own understanding. I want her beside me to talk about the big house, the yuppie neighborhood and the snacks rich people leave. The Post-its written in cursive encouraging the dogsitter to eat whatever they'd like. Gluten-free bread in the freezer. Natural almond milk bottled and stored upside down in the fridge. I imagine showing my wife shelves and shelves of food and us holding one another by the waist and feeding one another from our knuckles. When the woman asks if I'm going to serve her or what, I tell her I'm happy to help. I hear her eye roll more than I see it.

She snaps and points at her items: three plastic bags of nuts.

Oh, I say. I'm so sorry to tell you this, but you need to have a code to buy from the bulk section. I look around to see if this is a trick, a game show, a reality-TV segment, but everyone is looking at their own work shoes, bored and tired.

Look it up, she says. In your book.

Bulk-section codes aren't in our book, I say, certain now that she is the same woman who told me to fuck myself. Makeup and a ball cap work wonders to change a person. I hand her a pen and say, Do you mind going back and writing it down? She grips the pen and when I let go, she lets it fall. When it bounces onto the floor, I drop to my knees to grab it, desperate, as though I am someone who loves a pen with dark-blue ink.

When I stand, the mother is eating walnuts straight from the bag. Mouth open in a tease. I tell her those haven't been weighed yet, that I can't check her out properly if the weight isn't correct. Playacting, of course; we both know at this point she isn't going to pay for any of the nuts. I wonder if she's slipped cartons of guava juice or boxes of protein pancake mix into her stroller. I imagine her baby sitting pretty on squeezable organic applesauces.

I ask her what she wants from me; I do want to know this woman, I decide. I want to understand how she moves in this world outside the store. Does she treat everyone like a dog or is it an attitude she saves especially for me? I decide if we met on the app I would be very mean to her. She keeps eating from the bag and I tell her she'd better go—there are cameras in here. The store does prosecute for stealing, I say, and without a change of face, she steers her baby right the fuck away.

Once in the bathroom, I listen to a voicemail informing me I did not get the bakery shift—there's no invite to be trained as a substitute or to keep an eye out for new openings. I delete it and hope I never see that woman again; I feel that betrayed. I text Charlotte a picture of my nipples. She asks if I ever use. Thinking of my sober wife, I type: Who doesn't?

12

CHARLOTTE WANTS REASSURANCE FROM RE-becca, so when she does not immediately jump up from bed and greet her, she deflates. She feels small and unimportant and shaky. Bea is sitting at Rebecca's feet and Charlotte greets both of them by name when she lets herself in; her Rebecca never locks the door when she's home. Bea barks loudly.

I love her, Rebecca says dreamily, and Charlotte feels sick, thinking she means her ex-wife. She stares at her Rebecca, wanting to bolt, and hates herself for having to say, Who? Come on, she's thinking. If you're hurting me at least show me you're being intentional about it.

The plant, her Rebecca says, laughing. She's a bird-of-paradise, and the new love of my life.

That's funny, Charlotte says, not laughing.

Her Rebecca has hopeful eyes; Charlotte wonders

if she was missed in the time she spent with Other Rebecca. But she doesn't want to think about one while in the room with the other; it feels wrong. Her Rebecca says, What's gotten you so spooked?

Bea, Charlotte says, immediately regretting that answer. I meant to pick her up a puppy ice cream, she adds. And I'm annoyed with myself because I forgot, and so when I saw her, I had to face my shame. Her Rebecca says she loves the plant and so does Bea.

And it's fine for her, her Rebecca says carefully. If she does happen to get into it, right?

Totally, Charlotte says. She can't remember if she explicitly reminded Olivia about pet toxicity, but she knows all about her trials and tribulations with Bea. And besides, Charlotte thinks, animals survive the wild all the time.

I'm going to win you over, Charlotte tells the dog. Just you wait. Bea barks again and Charlotte hopes she isn't grimacing. It's not even Bea she wants; what Charlotte wants is a clean slate with Rebecca. She'd have Rebecca move in with her, but her mother doesn't allow her to have pets, and she knows Rebecca won't give up her sixty-pound furry Goliath.

Charlotte repeats herself and neither looks up. She says, Babe? And she senses Rebecca is on the verge of breaking up with her on the spot.

Rebecca hands her a sleek plastic folder. It's thick with paper and Charlotte wonders if it's from the family services agency. Charlotte has vague ideas about the whole process being like an adoption or surrogacy; she imagines photos of unhappy children holding donated toys, their eyes unfocused and filled with distrust. Charlotte hopes one of the children looks a little like herself and a little like her Rebecca. When she opens the folder, her fear is that only one child will look familiar, and it will look exactly like Rebecca's wife.

The pages are, in fact, a marked-up copy of their sugaring contract. Charlotte notices several handwriting styles, though the ink is all red.

Who wrote this, she says, pointing to marginalia without letting herself read it. She's thinking, of course, that the other Rebecca is sabotaging her happiness, but she's having trouble envisioning a coherent Rebecca. The Rebecca at the market seemed cold, indifferent; the Rebecca at the café seemed unhinged. What if Rebecca actually wants the responsibility of a baby? Charlotte thinks these women would be wise to just let Charlotte handle the decision-making herself.

My sponsor, Rebecca says. And a few other girls from group.

Charlotte murmurs that this makes sense. She's livid. Not so much that her partner shared such intimate details about their dynamic—including payment schedules, safe words, and hard and soft boundaries—but that the group analysis did not lean in her favor. Charlotte sees herself as inherently self-centered but not selfish, and she wishes the women in her life could accept the difference. I'm not evil, she's thinking. I just want you to want what I want when I want it.

Can I come to a meeting, Charlotte says. Or hang out?

Hang out, her Rebecca repeats. It isn't a hangout.

You know what I mean, Charlotte says, annoyed. You eat after, don't you?

We support one another's sobriety during activities, she says. It helps us not feel like our lives are over, that we can still do things without using.

And I can't come, like, help you stay accountable, Charlotte says. I can't, I don't know, get people waters with lemons?

No, Rebecca says.

Does anyone's partner ever come, Charlotte says slowly.

No, Rebecca says, moving her eyes to meet Bea's. This movement gives Charlotte her answer, and she folds her shoulders into herself. She could cry, she thinks, but she doesn't. She releases a breath. Charlotte can't imagine her Rebecca acting the way she's said she did when things went sour with her wife: the yelling, the pushing, the hiding behind dumpsters after bolting shoeless during a midnight fight. Charlotte tells herself to stop wanting to witness this woman at her worst. That's not the only way to let love in, she thinks, but she isn't sure she believes herself. She isn't sure she believes anyone.

I can't go to class, I can't go to meetings, I can't hang out after, I can't wear the—

Are you saying this because you want me to change my mind, her Rebecca says. What are you getting at?

Charlotte hears but doesn't register. It's as if her anger has placed her behind the camera and she's just recording, just being a loyal transcriptionist for the events of her life. Bea is a clay dog, gray with black buttons for eyes, and her

Rebecca has spiders waving goodbye from her hair, their legs at home on her scalp. She isn't in control.

I can't get what I want, Charlotte says. Her voice feels clipped and distant, like an automated recording. I don't get chances to make things right, I just get rejection after rejection after rejection. I do exactly what you want, Rebecca.

You don't have to, her Rebecca says. You should do what *you* want, not what *I* want.

I want what you want, she says. She is trying very hard not to flipperboard her entire life.

If you want what I want, her Rebecca says, what's the problem?

What's the problem, Charlotte repeats. She's confused now too. What is the problem?

You can leave, Rebecca says coolly. Surprising herself, Charlotte does.

YOU DON'T NEED to suffer like this, Olivia says. They're sitting side by side on the bleachers next to the market. Olivia drove over, picked up avocado sushi and edamame dumplings, two hazelnut lattes with banana milk, while Charlotte made her way down the street, sweaty feet in her black ballet flats, the other Rebecca on the phone, coaching her on how to breathe in a J shape, how to relax, how to finally, finally catch a fucking break.

I don't like being alone, Charlotte says. You know what I mean.

Charlotte, Olivia says. You are so alone.

Rebecca

13

I CONFIRM THE WOO-WOO CLASS WITHOUT TELL-ing Charlotte. I feel impulsive, weird; maybe she'll think I'm overeager, a crunchy know-it-all trying to control her body. My impulse to improve Charlotte's life is familiar to me—I can't understand why anyone would spend time with me, unless they are depressed and making bad decisions, and I feel guilty, indebted to these people, and I think maybe I am here to do something important, to serve a purpose. I'm walking to meet Charlotte in my wife's neighborhood, where she asked me to *pick her up*, as though I have more than just my body.

I think I see her down the block, wearing one of those patterned dresses with bright colors, like I imagine rich women do on the Cape. The event is donation based so I've snuck a five-dollar bill from a roommate's cluttered tote bag, should I be strong-armed at the door, and am scratching it against my wet fingers in the pockets of my shorts. The dress isn't meant for pregnant bellies, I think. The fabric is stretched tight and I imagine pulling a thread and unraveling her right there on the sidewalk. I feel like a pig.

She's carrying flowers and I recognize the twine and brown wrapping paper from my market, which makes me nervous—what if she's a customer? I feel grateful she didn't buy them when I was working. I bolt toward her and pretend to drive a car along the curb.

Ride's here, I yell. I put my hands on an imaginary steering wheel and squat in the middle of the sidewalk. I squint, giving myself an excuse to look at her a little longer. Unlike me, she's not wearing dollar flip-flops. Instead she wears platform tennis shoes that come looking smudged; a few customers talked about getting the style while vacationing in Italy, how careful the designers were with the scuff marks. She's half running, holding her belly with both hands. I wonder if the baby is annoyed.

Pour moi, Charlotte shouts. Her loudness surprises me as much as her eagerness to play along.

For two, I say. I wonder what the people driving by think, if there will be tweets about a pregnant woman being hijacked by a mime.

Charlotte holds her belly. She says, What about for three? I fix a face like I'm considering a lifetime with twins or at least a period of a life with them in the back seat of my pretend car. I tell her I can make an exception for an especially pretty lady and Charlotte crouches onto all fours right there on the sidewalk.

Her body is poised, agile. Comfortable. Her head stays tucked into her neck. For a second, I wonder what bugs come in blond. .

A dog, too, miss, I add, and she rolls her spine. I wonder if the baby feels lonely. When Charlotte charges me, her arms and legs out like arches, I make a show of slamming on the brakes. She rears her hips up like a deer and scuttles around me, palms flat to the ground and tiptoes in the back. It occurs to me we're going to be around a bunch of strangers and we're going to have to smile. I feel sick and small and terrified until Charlotte crawls up my legs with her front paws, her eyes squinted and focused on me.

Make way for dogs, I say. Ducklings, dancers, dandelions, daredevils, dragons . . .

Without a word, she bites my calf, all teeth and no lips. I don't expect tongue and I don't get it, either.

I stage-whisper *Is this going in the direction of a rabies shot* and Charlotte bites me harder and smiles. I ask her how she is feeling because it feels safer than asking what she is doing both in general and specifically with me. She says, Fine, and I look at her belly, thick like an enormous whitehead. She says she feels rejuvenated.

Really, I say. From the walking? She hasn't gotten up yet so I squat beside her.

I hate walking, she says. She's picking gravel from the pink meat of her hands and I'm worrying she's about to change her mind about our activity. If she asks for anything more than five dollars, I am going to have to saunter into traffic again.

Do you need to go home, I ask, trying to sound nonchalant. I understand if you need to rest . . .

I love to rest, she says. I love surprises more.

Surprises like pretending to be a dog, I say, and she purses her lips, as though I really have disappointed her. How I misunderstood her so deeply, I don't understand. Aren't we playing? Isn't this the point?

Add eight legs, she says, and I do.

I say, Ooh you're a spider, and she nods expectantly. I'm embarrassed, even though I'm the one standing, pretending to be normal.

No imagination, she chides, and I resolve to ace our wellness; she will be the most prepared birther the hospital has ever seen. It occurs to me I don't know where she is giving birth; is it actually a hospital, or one of those clinics? Her apartment? I hope she doesn't ask me to be there.

Get in, I tell her. I toss my head over my shoulder like cab drivers do in movies. Charlotte looks at me until my bones are embarrassed and I repeat myself, tell her if she's ungrateful, I'm sure I can find someone else to accompany me. I've got myself in order, squatting like a jerk, all eyebrows, ready to become another person.

Where, she says. Where are we going? She says she might need to pee. I reassure her there's a bathroom and she says she might need to go right now, actually, she's so sorry. I tell her I can't hear her stream from the sidewalk bushes but I do.

In my head we honk honk honk like that down the road. She's saying, Woo-hooo, and I'm honking like a horn. We're weird, I say eventually, in real life, and Charlotte tells me *I'm* weird and I say, Yeah *we* are, and she asks me to stop the car. I stop short and she hits me from behind. Her belly is dense. I fall forward and the drop feels good, like I've given my life over to someone who understands more than I do.

I don't always like *weird*, Charlotte says. She doesn't help me get up.

I feel like a rejected kid and tell her *I* like weird and we don't talk until we're at the door of the building. We don't get buzzed in right away, even though a couple of people in uniforms are talking in the lobby. I'm used to being unseen and I don't really mind it; I like having proof of the world conspiring against my best intentions. Charlotte steps around me, makes her pretty pregnant self visible, and suddenly the door is opening for us, and I walk in, feeling like a jackass for not getting the door or willing myself dead.

I point to a coffee and tea station in the lobby. Her eyes move all around the couches; there's a lot of canned sparkled water and those enormous jugs we sell at work ($44.99, reusable straw sold separately at $5.99) and manicured hands. Everyone is pregnant or touching a pregnant person. Everyone is looking at a screen.

Charlotte says, Surprise me. She seems slighter now that we're inside the lobby, timid; she doesn't want to be here, because I said something or did something. I want to die.

The machine is fancy and, to my great relief, familiar to me from the months I spent cleaning houses. What isn't familiar to me is how to make a drink safe for pregnant people. Asking Charlotte directly is too risky; I've already managed to upset her. My body feels tight and tired with anxiety. When will a muumuu-ed someone ask for donations? Better yet, when will someone take my breath away and hold it for me? I pretend to read the label of a sugar-free vanilla coffee syrup and wait for someone else to make a cup.

How far along are we, a person asks. I continue staring at the mug I've grabbed; hand-painted strawberries and cherries, from a local artist that did a pop-up in the store's entryway last summer. They cost thirty dollars each.

It's not for me, I say, and put on my best clueless face. This person seems helpful, eager; *matronly* comes to mind, though I don't know if that word is inherently a pejorative.

Is the drinker pregnant, the person asks. The name tag reads ORGANIZER 3.

Yes, I say. I think so.

The organizer seems amused, but too focused. I can't begin to guess how far along Charlotte is, and I can't figure out the right way to ask. Talking about her body feels like an imposition. Don't we all want to be ourselves without explanation? I tell the woman the drinker wants a surprise.

Organizer 3 works magic. I wonder if she actually works at a café, maybe makes coffee at five in the morning, maybe is the first face people see besides their own. She scoops a fragrant dark-brown mixture into the mug.

Hot water next. She mentions a nice roasted flavor, rich. The mug feels hot in my hand; I worry I'm going to fall forward, trip over my feet, burn someone's face or fetus. I ask if it's decaf, whatever it is, and she says it's a naturally decaffeinated malted barley. Plus a little chicory—don't believe the hysteria, a little is just fine for both mother and baby! I repeat this explanation in my head until I'm back to Charlotte, who is curled up on a couch with a pillow to her chest.

Barley with lots of milk and honey, she repeats, miserably. It sounds like a vegan ice cream flavor. I like matcha, she says. Remember? The café?

That's an eleven-dollar pint, I tell her, and she says we should get some. I malfunction a little, a terrible crumbling in my face; having to tell Charlotte it's not a real possibility, it's too indulgent, ruins my effort in trying to make her happy. It's about the effort, not the delivery. It occurs to me I wouldn't have to clarify to my wife I'd been teasing, playacting, as she has been poor with me long enough.

Charlotte scrunches her nose. She nods. I feel foolish, skittish; nothing is on my mind but feeling safe with Charlotte and the child I haven't yet met but already feel a duty to respect. I repeat my story about the organizer and her fixing the cup.

I asked you for a surprise, Charlotte says unhappily.

I panicked, I say. I don't add I'm sorry, though I am, because my wife has begged me to find something more honest and specific than my apologies.

So that's what you like, she says unhappily. Being told

what to do? It's so easy, Rebecca. It's boring. She talks like she's had this conversation many times.

We don't have to go upstairs, I offer. We can take a walk. I am always willing to give up on plans to keep a person happy and, preferably, with me. Everything about this feels wrong. I'm torn between bolting to my wife's and blocking Charlotte on all mediums. What am I even doing? People are heading upstairs, the line for the elevator is dwindling. I suggest trying this another day.

Because I'm irritable, Charlotte says. I'm a monster so I'm missing out. She seems near tears, too.

You're pregnant, I tell her. Not a monster.

If I weren't pregnant, she says slowly, would my emotions be a big deal?

If you weren't pregnant, I tell her, would you be here? We get in line for the elevator.

Charlotte

14

CHARLOTTE CLOCKS THE WELLNESS CLASS AS A multi-level marketing scheme within minutes of arrival at the shabby apartment building. The organizers flicker around the foyer, charming the doormen, corralling the bellies and belly-less partners. Others seem to act as their assistants, filming the scene with their phones and following up with pregnant-appearing people about dietary needs. Charlotte is suspicious, guarded—she's sure all these people have already had babies. She puts her hands on top of her belly and thumbs her sternum.

Did you give these people our information, she asks in the elevator. She's feeling irritable, on edge after her latest roller coaster with her Rebecca. There are a few other people in the elevator with them, all quiet. Listening. At Rebecca's blank face, Charlotte asks if Rebecca gave them her insurance information (no), either of their last names (no), social security numbers (no), phone numbers (no), or her due date (no).

They asked how many people were coming and I put two adults and one fetus, she says. Rebecca's panicked already, shifting from foot to foot and looking to the door. If she had been prepared, Charlotte would have made up her face differently, given herself under-eye circles and a proper bloat. Coming clean doesn't enter her mind.

The elevator opens.

You included the fetus, Charlotte says in the hall. Rebecca nods, poor eye contact and a sheepish face, like she's just a kid who doesn't know what she's doing, a little girl trying every knob in a long hallway. Charlotte lowers her voice and says she needs to hear an honest answer, okay, and Rebecca does her puppy-eye nod, who me, and, to Charlotte's delight, begins to play with her hair, twisting it around her fingers.

You're a puppy, Charlotte thinks. You're so easy to read.

Woof, this Rebecca says. Woof.

Rebecca, Charlotte says. Is this a cult? She feels excited. Will they be in a documentary? A long-form investigative feature?

I don't know, Rebecca says. Why would it be a cult?

So many pregnant people, Charlotte says. So many herbal teas. Rebecca says nothing so Charlotte repeats herself: So many pregnant people, so many herbal teas, and Rebecca says, Hmm, and Charlotte prods, asks Rebecca what makes her so sure this is the right fit for them.

I was drawn in by the pictures, Rebecca admits. Healthy breathing diagrams.

Did you sign up for a package? A series of classes.

No . . .

How much is it per class?

It's donation based, Rebecca says. Like an introduction to wellness.

You found it how, Charlotte says. She feels excited and warm, eager when Rebecca hands over her phone. Craigslist is pulled up. There's a long listing for a natural eco-friendly allergen-free pregnancy support circle meeting in this apartment building twice a month on Sunday. *In lieu of church*, the listing reads. *Honor the salvation you carry.*

It's actually free, this Rebecca mumbles. I just thought . . .

You found this for me, Charlotte says slowly. You went searching.

The women sit in a circle. They're in a small living room with rugs spread over a faux wood floor. Instrumental music with ads plays from somebody's laptop. Charlotte realizes there's no air conditioner, just two fans attempting a crosswind. She suddenly worries these people are sovereign citizens, off-the-grid types who don't want any medical intervention. She looks down and sees her belly is a lump of big blue clay. No air slicing.

I'm a little warm, Charlotte says, and Rebecca hauls

ass to ask after ice. A little more alone, Charlotte considers all the bellies around her: smooth D shapes and bubbled Bs. Charlotte always goes for a D shape, pretty and smooth.

Charlotte watches the women furiously type on their phones. At least one person tries calling someone saved as HUBBY until she puts her phone face down and goes to the bathroom. Charlotte wonders how the woman is feeling, what's happening in her body, does she feel the need to burn down the building? Does she feel dramatically unloved, unsaved, unremembered? A blimp with a parasite, all while some person is out and about, falling in love with some younger, prettier, less-pregnant model? Charlotte doesn't see the woman reenter the room.

The organizers sit at three points of the circle, with Charlotte directly across from her personal nemesis, Organizer 3. Rebecca stands over her, asking if she needs a pillow or another tea, and Charlotte asks questions— have the pillows been sprayed with a scent? Are they decorative? This Rebecca shrugs and shrugs, squirms around on her feet, all brown puppy eyes. Charlotte sees this Rebecca as an old woman, grayed and ambivalent, scurrying around and fetching things. She feels warm and content, momentarily matured.

Finally the room quiets and Charlotte whispers at Rebecca to sit down. Be like everyone else, Charlotte thinks, mean, this Rebecca runs anxious, runs desperate, like she's the one person on earth breathing without permission, all stolen air.

Here, she says. She pats her lap. This Rebecca puts

her head on Charlotte's thighs, face into her stomach, nose flat up against the truth. Charlotte stills, waits; most people would ask to hear the baby, to feel the kicks and punches. This Rebecca is so inside herself, she doesn't even put her ear to the belly. Charlotte wonders if this is how her Rebecca got away with drinking so much and for so long; it's not hard to hide what no one is looking for.

No boring introductions here, Organizer 1 says. We embrace the inner child.

A little game, Organizer 2 says. People love it.

We're next to the couple to beat, a woman next to them whispers, giggling. The woman is thinner than Charlotte, closer to Olivia, upsetting her, especially since she's actually pregnant. She squints. Probably actually pregnant. Charlotte wonders what she'll look like pushing. The probably pregnant person's partner looks aloof, stressed; he stares at her body for too long, and Charlotte gives a smile that's hardly more than a scowl. You're wasting time, Charlotte wants to tell the woman. You're squandering what's special.

Due dates, the leader says. Projected astrology is also permissible. Everyone giggles, including the men, including sad-eyed Rebecca, her hehehe dropping from Charlotte's middle to her vulva.

No gender reveal, someone says. No assigned-gender-at-birth reveal, rather. Everyone nods, and most in the group give a month and day, an approximation of life changing. Charlotte feels superior, momentarily good—she doesn't have an end date, doesn't have anyone or anything pulling her happiness out from inside her.

I'm Charlotte the Controller, she says. And I don't want to know, Charlotte says. All surprises here. She hopes for laughs and speaks into silence instead.

How do you schedule maternity leave, the woman next to her says. Your bosses have not asked?

Charlotte imagines spraying the woman with citrus lavender peppermint oil mint cinnamon vinegar eucalyptus. Go away, she's thinking. Shrivel up.

Baby's nice and high, someone says. You know what that means . . .

First pregnancy, the woman beside Charlotte says. She's becoming a moth in Charlotte's eye, an insect. Abdominal wall is probably still tight.

We come in all shapes and sizes, the leader says. Nothing indicates sex.

I'm Rebecca the rat, Rebecca says, and everybody laughs.

You could be carrying a dead baby, the moth-woman says, and Charlotte realizes she is serious. You might think you're the luckiest girl in the world, and . . .

Sorry, the moth's partner, a larva, says. We've been having a little pre-birth anxiety.

You need to make an appointment, the moth says. Let us help you.

I am the luckiest girl in the world, Charlotte says. But thank you, you're very kind. She hopes if she speaks calmly, if she fixes her face just right, she can be this adored the rest of the hour.

The moth waits.

Did it happen to you, Charlotte says, and Rebecca stills, her face looking mortified. I can ask this, Charlotte is thinking. This is the one time I can ask this.

Did you think you had something special, Charlotte says. Did you keep something so safe you ruined it?

The moth opens her mouth. Charlotte peers down her throat and counts eggs. Dozens, hundreds. Small, elongated ovals. The moth wiggles, sends her belly side to side, and Charlotte spies squirming white larvae and cocoons. A whole ecosystem, she thinks. Dark and safe and quiet.

You've got the whole enchilada, Charlotte says, and the moth closes her mouth around Charlotte's head, dark and safe and quiet.

I THINK THEY'RE tenderqueers, Other Rebecca says when Charlotte comes to in the hallway. Her head feels fuzzy, like she's just acted for many hours. They're sitting side by side on a sticky leather couch. I *think* that's what happened. They're astrology queers. That's why it felt so . . .

Judgy, Charlotte says. Culty. She's holding her belly very tightly. She can't remember exactly where things went wrong; she has a lifelong habit of holding her breath until she passes out, something born in childhood she can't quite let go of.

That's why they were so intense about . . . the due date, Charlotte says. Controlling.

Us against them, Rebecca says seriously, and Charlotte feels animated, enlivened. Is this what her Rebecca has been hinting at? This Rebecca, always ready to bite a moving target. Charlotte feels the viewfinder widen and widen, her scene broadening from a room to the planet.

15

MY WIFE HAS TWO CANDLES LIT, WHITE WEDDING cake and crème brûlée. I'm feeling adrenalized and remorseful; guilty for having just seen Charlotte, though I don't know if I'll ever see her again, if our little affair will end before it's consummated. I want Charlotte to leave me so I can focus on my wife and I want Charlotte to consume my thoughts so I stay the hell away from the marriage I've already left. Just as I did when I actually lived there, I asked my wife if she had been baking.

Rebecca tells me no, and tilts her head to the candles on the table. I make a show of leaning over and sniffing in the heat. Rebecca sits on the bed, feet hanging off the side, and Beatrice rubs her ankles with the side of her mouth. I wonder if Rebecca can feel her teeth or if she only parts her lips that way for me.

Without getting up, Rebecca tells me there's water in

the pitcher if I'm thirsty. I tell her I am and offer to pour her a glass. She accepts and as I walk into her kitchen (our kitchen) she tells me there's no ice. There hasn't been a reason, she says. The tension between us dictates the air, the way the room breathes.

The familiarity of the cabinets and drawers makes me queasy. I want to drop beneath the floorboards and nap. I want to curl up in the corner of a dusty ceiling, borrow space from a mother spider, and watch Rebecca and the dog stream reality television. As I pour myself water, I wonder how difficult it would be to set up a ladder outside and watch their happiness through a window. If I fell, I think, I would die.

Why don't you have groceries, I say without turning around. The fridge is emptier than we kept it before I left. Mustard ketchup egg-free mayonnaise balsamic glaze apple ranch gone. A big tub of hummus sits in the center of the top shelf. Carrots and bell peppers shrivel in the crisper. Shelves appear clear of fingerprints and I wonder if she emptied and scrubbed the place in an effort to be rid of me. Only bananas on the stovetop seem fresh. I repeat myself and ask if she's been out of town or something.

I haven't had much appetite, she says. Come watch with me, she adds. It's our show.

I sit on the floor and look at her when she's looking at her laptop screen. We chuckle while couples flub question after question in a game designed to show how much they know about one another. In my head, I nail the game: wife's favorite apple (Gala); wife's favorite type of physician (endocrinologist); wife's favorite place to experience rain (the coast during winter). I worry these couples are destined to fail and worry even more so that this experience will bleed into our relationship. Over and over, I think: Is my wife sitting here, watching these losers, thinking we are so similar to these people? Failures, failures.

When the next episode queues, I tell her I have a gift card for delivery. She asks where I got it and I consider lying and saying it was a thank-you from work for doing such a good job, but I remember she is still my Rebecca, and she will be more impressed to hear the truth. She dotes on me—*good eyes!!*—and I suggest the Thai place she loves and we're hovering over her laptop together, pretending to consider all the options, even the new stuff. I'm thinking I don't need to see Charlotte again to be happy. I'm thinking my wife loves me again.

She tells me to just stay on the bed, the floor is so hard, and when the food comes, I vacate just long enough to retrieve the bags before we sit beside the bed together to eat. She tells me she hates when the pillows smell like dinner, as though I didn't know that from day one.

The dog resists when I sit back on the bed. Black eyes hang on my movements like she doesn't care for me but wants to know what the hell I am up to. I can't blame her. Beatrice is not a biter, never has been, either, and yet I defer to her. She hasn't forgiven me yet, I say to my wife. No one has forgiven me, not really; not my wife and not myself. I am temporary, playacting, a transition. Rebecca still has not brought up her scheme or the paperwork or feelings for me outside of tolerating my presence. I ask her again why she is barely eating. I tell her I'm worried.

You're one to talk, she says. She tells me she's allowed to be sad. I am too cowardly to ask if she wants to talk about real things, deep things, the things I think about all the time, and when Beatrice nips my fingers, I keep patting her back, happy to accept acknowledgment when it comes.

When we finish eating, I put the plates in the sink and wash them with dish soap and hot water. I do not use gloves. When we lived together, I resisted dishes and accepted the smell that took over the apartment. Rebecca did them for years until she stopped. I wanted to spoon more and more into her mouth, to keep filling her, but did not want to risk her bite. I let the water run until my fingers ache. As I dry my hands on the bottom of my shirt, I play Heads or Tails, Heads or Tails, and settle on Heads, I'm getting what I want.

I ask Rebecca if she has anything for burns. Not my hands, I say. Some coffee spilled on me the other day.

Shit, she says. Coffee? She tells me she's always had a bad feeling about that market. It's true, she has. I got the job right around the time I left; I felt too ashamed to return to the pharmacy after missing two consecutive shifts on account of being catatonic and unwashed in bed.

When I nod in agreement she heads into the bathroom and I hear rummages in the medicine cabinet. I remember the first aid kit her mother bought us when we first moved in together, years ago. We never really used it but it seems Rebecca did not toss it along with so much else. She tells me she'll check the skin and clean it for me and when I resist, she tells me to get over myself. There's nothing about you I haven't seen, she says. There's nothing I don't know. I say, Same to you, and remind myself to check the medicine cabinet for nips before I go.

This is nuts, I tell her. But I got hit by a car, too.

She says, Okay, like she thinks I'm joking, and whenever she realizes the truth I offer her, she doesn't point out her shift in perception.

With my shirt off, Rebecca is all business. Her phone serves as a flashlight and she homes in on the skin on my shoulder and chest. If she is aroused by my marigold sports bra, she does not mention or suggest it. My wife asks if a customer spilled the coffee on me and I am careful in my reply. I know if I blame a customer, she will take my side, but too much so—she will encourage me to sue. If I blame a coworker, she will say the same. So I tell her a variation of the truth, that yes, the coffee was at work, but it was my own fault. I poured myself a cup and left it on the edge of a counter, stood up too fast, and knocked it on myself. She dabs at my skin with a moist cloth as I explain myself, worrying if I am giving a touch too much detail. She tells me we should dig the aloe vera out from the beach bag and put it in the fridge. The cool will be good on your skin, she says.

In the bedroom closet, I lean into her hung tops—sweaters and hoodies and crewnecks and four blazers, nice ones we found at the thrift store for teaching and interviews—and breathe. My breaths are bad. Shallow, small. Scurrying. If I were another person, I might cry. I imagine myself weeping, the relief of it, and the confusion, too. Rebecca might feel torn about comforting me, might ask me to leave or to stay. I want nothing I express to change the course of anyone's life, not even my own. Returning to this home repeats a question I still do not know the answer to: Why did I leave? I was unhappy; we were unhappy. She was drunk and I was nervous. Obsessive. Controlling. I consider the fridge, the dog, the floor, and the nips. We, I think, are all still unhappy.

Rebecca calls my name from the kitchen and I know she is watching from across the room. I get on my knees and root through the luggage and totes on the floor, pull out the sticky aloe bottle, tell her it's all good. My hands make quick work and I don't feel round glass piled beneath faded backpacks—either she's changed her hiding spot or she's really stopped, and with less than five hundred square feet to work with, I find myself hoping.

It's still all good, I think, when I return to the fridge and add the aloe to the empty side shelf, where we used to store sriracha and soy sauce and mustard and lemon juice. We kissed with the fridge door open, again and again, in that apartment and the spaces we'd lived in before. We were good at finding those transitional moments, the life lived in a single doorway. Opportunities to acknowledge each other's bodies and our own. It's all still good, I think, when she tells me to just come to bed and to just stay.

With the TV on, I sit on the bed beside my wife. The dog sits between us. She watches my concentrated stillness, my face on the small screen. If it were winter, I'm sure I would still be wearing my coat and I'm equally sure my wife knows it. She instructs me again to just stay and I do until morning when I wake beside my wife to hear Bea whining for release.

She needs to go out, I tell her. I can do it. We're good at this, I am thinking. Solving other people's little problems. Remember? She murmurs her assent and when I fiddle with her collar and put on my wife's sneakers, my brain feels empty, happy. Automatic, easy. It's just before seven in the morning and I watch a woman squat and piss in the parking lot. On her face, an enormous joy.

While the dog sits on the cement, I sit beside her. The ground feels damp through my leggings. I pat my thighs and tell the dog my body is more comfortable and she ignores me, so I pat, pat, pat and she gives me eyes before she settles herself in a circle, head on my knees. I wonder if she's had accidents in the hallway lately and if she resents me for being one less person to help her. I tell her I am sorry for leaving, sorry for changing, or for trying to, and that I am sad and stupid and confused. I ask her if she wants me to come home and of course she does not answer. I begin to lift myself to stand and she presses her nails into the fat above my knees. From the cement, I watch house sparrows pick at fallen seeds and like to think she's telling herself to remember this morning, too.

My wife and I held hands in the night, long enough that I almost fell asleep, over and over, and drifted enough to remind myself to remember. Our bodies treated each other to that safest heat. Early into the evening, when we agreed our eyes hurt and the laptop closed, I wondered if we might have sex or something like it, but we did not. I did not let myself think about our actions, as curious as I was, so observant of both myself and of my wife. I kept thinking that I had nothing to compare this to; I was never one to get back with exes, to hook up with old dates. The dog tells me when it's time to get up, and we do, and when we're inside, my wife is rushing to get ready. She looks nice—really nice. Had I gotten so used to her I'd forgotten how she appears to strangers? Or she's lost the alcohol puff. Her eyes are back.

I have office hours at ten, she says, and I guess she feels she owes me an explanation or an excuse. She asks if I took the ChapStick this morning and I tell her no. Later, when I am gone, I wish I had, as I cannot remember if it was coconut raspberry blueberry vanilla brown sugar or cinnamon. Later, when I kiss Charlotte, I taste her and do not remember my wife's taste but know, for certain, that it is different.

Charlotte

16

CHARLOTTE'S MOTHER DECORATED HER APART-
ment. The living room walls are sage and the love seats
are turquoise. There's a half-empty bookshelf built into
the wall and tall windows. Charlotte sometimes worries
she's the only lesbian millennial in the city with floor-
length curtains, but she knows her mother will simply
have them replaced if she manages to get them down
herself. There's one cream rug alongside several gray and
white area ones arranged by a delicate science Charlotte
cannot quite understand but appreciates objectively.
Charlotte confesses her mother's influence when the
other Rebecca enters, admitting her mom reviews her
credit card charges each month.

She didn't want me to look all new money, Charlotte
says, the words feeling funny in her mouth. Isn't that
terrible?

Totally, Rebecca says, looking bored.

Charlotte makes a show of leaning over her dining room table, ostensibly to grab a pitcher of water but really to show Rebecca her breasts. She's thinking: Don't be unhappy don't be unhappy. Her desire to be desired shames her almost as much as her ongoing charade of being pregnant. When Rebecca comes around the table and puts her hands on Charlotte's hips, she's willing Rebecca to cradle her stomach, but she doesn't.

You've done this before, Rebecca says quietly. Right?

Of course, Charlotte says. She doesn't know what this Rebecca is referring to but internally rattles off a number of possibilities: sex, sex with women, sex with the belly. She figures two out of three truths isn't bad. Rebecca licks her neck and earlobes for a while and Charlotte tries to figure out how to keep Rebecca from taking Charlotte's shirt off. She could pretend there's a fire or a masked man in the doorway. She could get Olivia to call or stop by. But she does want to sleep with Rebecca. She sighs out of frustration with herself and Rebecca freezes.

Tell me, she says. What's wrong?

My back, Charlotte lies. It's so sore.

Rebecca steps back and sits on the table. She leans forward to put her head against Charlotte's stomach and Charlotte lets her. She's thinking: Please don't notice please don't notice please don't notice. Rebecca rolls herself up and Charlotte smiles broadly.

Did they get bigger, Rebecca says.

What, Charlotte says. She sniffs. How do good

intentions spoil so quickly? She wonders if either Rebecca likes banana bread.

Your breasts, Rebecca says. Are you pumping them, or something? Already?

Charlotte considers this question for a single moment before saying yes, she's been working to induce lactation to build up a supply, this lesbian she follows online has a whole series about getting milk ready and putting it in a deep freezer in her garage before the baby is born, as she won't have a partner and her family thinks she's a sinner. The woman is ugly, which is unfortunate, as Charlotte would've probably hit her up. She isn't entirely lying; she *has* used a pump on herself while masturbating. But in reality, she's ovulating and her hormones are likely the root of her maybe-increased breast size.

Rebecca appears to consider this response before saying, Hot. Then she tugs open Charlotte's bra and puts her nipple inside her mouth.

Charlotte straightens her shoulders and puts her hands on Rebecca's waist, then drops them back to her own sides. She'd put them on her lap but then they'd still be on Rebecca, who is dangerously close to resting on her belly. Women have sucked Charlotte's breasts before to varying degrees of pleasure, but this experience feels tilted upside down. Don't compare them, she's thinking. But of course, she does compare them.

This Rebecca is less restrained than her Rebecca, despite their relative lack of emotional intimacy. This worries Charlotte, as she's long feared that the cornerstones of good relationships—honesty, reliability, caretaking—correlate with unexciting sex. She puts her hands on Rebecca's head.

You're super hot, Rebecca says before switching breasts.

Thank you, Charlotte says. The power titillates her until she watches Rebecca pop her nipple out of her mouth, hold up a finger to signal a pause, and flips around. Charlotte tries to tell her this position seems unstable; I don't want you to fall, ha!, but Rebecca assures her she can just hold on to her stomach. Charlotte titters.

I'm kidding, Rebecca says. My feet are flat on this chair. She kicks a little and the chair squeaks against the floor.

Cool, Charlotte says. She is pretty sure she is about to cry from stress.

The belly is an anchor, Rebecca says before resuming. Keeps me stable.

Charlotte feels a little pride. Her belly is an anchor. Could it be a flotation device? Maybe. Her belly could rescue a very small dog or cat or lizard from a dirty whirlpool for sure. Or like, a 50 percent chance. Her belly's not a real baby, no, but it's not nothing. She wills herself to relax but her stomach hurts. You're ashamed, she thinks. You're so fucking stupid.

Shame is nothing new for Charlotte, both in general and specific to her body. Olivia's face watches from the ceiling and Charlotte resists her desire to give her the finger. She's never been able to relax in her own home, but imagined surveillance is a new low. It's because you're a liar, she thinks. You dummy. Her Rebecca's face replaces

Olivia's on the ceiling. She looks sad, Charlotte thinks. Resigned. What Charlotte wants to see is herself running toward her, her double, a mirror, desperate, effusive. She shudders.

Be right back, Other Rebecca says before sliding off the table. Charlotte reflexively covers her breasts then flinches. Her skin is red and tender. There isn't much spit. She's touching her fingertips to her nipples when she hears the ice machine gurgle.

My mom keeps reminding me to fix that, she blurts. Rebecca mocks her, all contorted: *my mom keeps reminding me to fix that* and Charlotte throws a soft banana at her. Rebecca shields herself with her glass of ice.

You almost took out my eye, she says, and Charlotte feels a funny happiness. We're not performing, she thinks. With her hands on her breasts, she darts to retrieve the banana, and Rebecca stops her easily. Hey, she says. Miss me?

You don't know how to fix that, either, Charlotte says. Rebecca winces and admits she's right, she has no idea how to fix that ice maker. But she can look it up.

I don't care about the ice machine, Charlotte says. I care about me.

Charlotte sits between Rebecca's legs on the floor. Rebecca ices her breasts and Charlotte masturbates into the palm of her hands a little. She prefers this position as the angle hides her double chin. Charlotte wishes she remembered a time she felt at home in her body, but childhood memories are dim. Puberty superseded them, she thinks; her period started the first in her group of friends, and she developed breasts quickly. Her mother sexualized her growth more than anyone, nitpicking at the cut of her T-shirts and always making Charlotte raise her arms to see if bra straps showed. Remnants of Liv's eating disorders—thinned hair, anemia, and digestive pain—still mess up her life, but Charlotte nonetheless envies Liv's small breasts and shapeless hips.

Up, Rebecca says. Come on. She tickles Charlotte's stomach, causing Charlotte to freeze up. Try standing up, Rebecca continues. I want to see the view. She laughs hot air into Charlotte's ear but Charlotte is too stricken to chuckle along. How many times can Rebecca not notice the belly is fake? How much time does she have? She worries Rebecca already knows and all the sweetness is an attempt to humiliate her.

I think I'm freaking out, she says quietly, and Rebecca stills.

Do you need a break, she says. I can go.

No, she says. Don't do that.

Something's wrong, Rebecca says. The focus in her voice surprises Charlotte; Rebecca reflexively reaches toward self-blame and the narcissism that comes with thinking you're the root of everybody's hurt. She adds, Tell me.

It's nothing, Charlotte says once or twice, and Rebecca repeats herself too: tell me tell me tell me. Charlotte says she gets funny about her stomach being touched.

You feel tokenized, Rebecca fills in. Like the baby is

for everybody else. She stutters out an apology for not asking for more explicit permission and Charlotte wonders if she's always been so quick to take the blame or if it's from the dregs of her relationship with the other Rebecca. Charlotte can't imagine her Rebecca acting in a way that would necessitate such quick self-flagellation, but that's exactly what she wants to witness: the explosion.

No, Charlotte says. It's just, like normal stuff.

What's normal stuff, Rebecca says.

Like ... my weight, she says. You know, my body changing. And you'll see, she continues. Liv? She's like, skinny skinny. It's a whole thing.

What do you mean, Rebecca says. A whole thing?

Charlotte doesn't really want to talk about Olivia or her body because it humiliates her, but she leans into the attention she's getting and describes some of their teen and college years, the two of them siloed as opposites: Olivia (small, skinny, vaguely elegant) and Charlotte (loud, child-bearing hips, try-hard). That both women were gay didn't seem to change how they were perceived and the way they moved in their bodies.

I'm really sorry, Rebecca says. I know you'll keep changing, but I wouldn't change you.

Charlotte nods and takes a moment to process the depths of her comfort; Rebecca's assuming Charlotte is going to have more bodily changes after birth, of course, and she's at least hinting she'll stick around for saggy skin and temporary adult diapers. It's the sort of comfort and loyalty she's always fantasizing about and yet she feels unwell. You feel sick because you are sick, she thinks. Because it's a lie of your own making.

To Rebecca, she turns and kisses her on the mouth and says, Open up. Rebecca swallows the melted cube like a snake.

17

I'M STONED BECAUSE CHARLOTTE WANTED TO chill out before we meet up with her friend Olivia. Charlotte repeats that Liv is a real artist; she's living off humanities grants, and I'm impressed enough to be mortified. What do I know about art? Like an angel, Charlotte seems to sense my dread and offers me drugs. I almost tell her she's like my wife, so good at knowing my needs.

We'd have split the weed—a brownie she got from another artist at the clay studio, who is *good for it*, according to Charlotte—but we're worried about the baby—or *I'm* worried about the baby; Charlotte seemed willing to scarf until I said something, and then her face got all touched and rosy—and I'm higher than shit on a nice bite. I feel happy, loose. Before I recognized my wife's addiction, I loved drinking with her, sneaking into tastings and sipping leftover cups of expensive reds. Booze makes me nervous, but the weed feels goofy, soft, like a daffodil growing from my earwax.

She's like, the best friend I've ever had because I've known her the longest, Charlotte says. But Liv makes me nervous. I ask if they were ever a thing and she says no, no, not like that. Charlotte feels like my wife in some of the best ways: she runs down her friend's life like she's catching me up on the first season of a show I missed but everyone else binged. Grew up with horses (equestrian, not farm); estranged from her parents (homophobic moderates); enjoys micro farm-to-table tasting menus (the ideal cover for a lifelong eating disorder); and has a disorganized attachment style. Charlotte hesitates then adds that Olivia can be a stickler for healthy food, but only sometimes.

It's a problem, Charlotte adds. We're holding hands on the brick sidewalk and anyone could see us. I tell her I have the solution to every problem and she asks me to please not sleep with her friend. I tell her I can promise at least that much and when we end up stuck behind a straight couple waiting to cross the street, she brings my hand to her breasts. I squeeze.

We walk to her friend's place in Georgetown and I try to calm myself down; the buildings here are nice nice, so nice I've never been inside one. How does an artist afford this? These aren't World Bank places—these are old money places. I try to comfort myself with a re-minder that at least these places are too old to support air-conditioning in the summers, but once we get up to

Olivia's one-bedroom, I realize she does, indeed, have central air-conditioning.

Oh, I say. Shit. I wonder if she's in on sugaring, too.

Forget something, Olivia asks. She's eyeing me like she knows I'm the type to show up empty-handed but Charlotte swoops her arms around me from behind and reveals a bouquet.

Rebecca picked them out, she says, though of course I didn't. They're from a farm in western Maryland, I announce too loudly, but Olivia seems pleased. She tells me she loves white and I say I can tell; her apartment is a chic minimalist dream, all subway tile and white walls. Except for the big wall of mirrors above her couch—those are portals to another dimension where my face is upside down and my eyes are bleeding. I stare dead into a small round mirror hung just above eye level and see my wife's legs kicking through my eyeholes. The impact in my head comforts me—I miss her.

It used to be brick in here, Olivia says when she nudges me into her kitchen. But my parents let me redo it when I moved it.

Did they live here before you, I say. Olivia, I'm reminding myself, isn't supposed to know I'm on drugs, and I can't remember why; did we not have enough for Olivia or is she sober? Don't ask about the mirrors, I think. Don't ask about the portals.

My mom used this as her painting studio, she says. But we actually lived outside the city. She tells me to hold the flowers over the sink while she trims the stems and I do. I think she could do some serious damage to me with those garden scissors. From behind us, Charlotte says we look like a couple.

Should I be jealous, she says, and I hope she has a good place to hook up in mind. The rooftop, I bet, has a fire pit and a view of the Kennedy Center all lit up.

That depends on how well she can cook, Olivia says, and I realize all the good I smelled is coming from a series of candles. The smell sours to me—I miss my wife, my favorite cook.

I say, Cook? I hope Charlotte knows I can't be responsible with holding a plate, much less a flame or knife. Maybe she wants us to hurt her, I think, then shudder—who is us? I imagine my wife kicking out of my eyes and standing beside me in the kitchen. Does Charlotte want us to destroy her? No, I want to destroy myself. I want my wife and me to destroy me. I imagine Charlotte taking better care of my wife and baby than I can and my stomach feels very long and low.

I don't want to kill us, I say. The women laugh at me until I join them.

We're going to *cook together*, Olivia says, enunciating as though speaking to a precocious child. And we need to get *ingredients*, too, and some *wine*. Char didn't tell you?

Char, I repeat, and Charlotte smacks her friend a little hard.

I hate that nickname, she says. Only Olivia can use it.

And your parents, she says. And your *mémère*. I must look confused because she adds, That means *grandmother*, and both women laugh.

Right, I say. Totally. Olivia tells me to hold the flowers

while she gets a vase out and of course I cut myself on a thorn. The flowers are holding little people—fairies, I guess—who look like my wife and who want me to sacrifice my throat so my wife can speak to us. Us being full-sized people. I swipe my fingers against the thorns until one sticks. I hope it's good enough but the fairies just return to water drops.

It's been a long time since I've let myself be fucked-up with other people; with Rebecca, I made sure to stay sober to keep an eye on her and make sure the fuckups we hung around didn't try to make a move or worse. But the weed's got me feeling out of my body. I'm away from it all, powerful and detached. I feel like a god or at least a decent person. Olivia takes the flowers from me and I'm sure she sees my bloody finger but she doesn't mention it and I wait until she's turned around to put my cut to Charlotte's mouth. She sucks in and we giggle all the way to Olivia's car, which appears to be an enormous black hole in the sidewalk.

It's been so long since I've been in a car like this, I say, and Olivia jumps on me. You mean a Tesla, she says. I've actually never been in one before; I let Charlotte manage the flashy door handle. And also because the car's interior has changed—it was black, then a gray mist, then a white shine that terrifies me because I do want to stay living.

Instead of filling them in on this scene, I tell Olivia, I just walk everywhere because of the environment. A half lie, but not a bad one, as Charlotte mmms and says she doesn't regret giving up her car to live in the city most of the time but drivers make it a real headache sometimes.

Always all, Oh are you going to see your boyfriend, oh is your husband waiting for you, and I'm like, trying to decide if it's worth getting killed over, she says, and I tell her she's so right, and it's such a pain to never get out where you actually live, even when it's raining, because you never know if they're going to circle back for you. Those were concerns I had more when Rebecca and I lived together full-time and blew money on Ubers to get her drunk self home, but still.

Olivia almost pulls into the store I work in but I save myself. I don't want to freak anyone out, I start, and she hovers in the entrance to the parking garage. No one's behind us and she looks over her shoulder as I speak. But I've heard there are actually rats in this one, it's a whole problem.

That sounds like a rumor, she says. I mean, they'd get like, shut down by the board of health.

Actually, I continue. It's an ongoing issue. In my head, I'm between two wild worlds: one in which I see and hear about the rats three or four mornings a week, when I open at the registers and watch the produce department smack the sides of big brown boxes until rodents scurry out. The rats move on their own time. My other world is a show just for me: human-sized rats waiting to usher us inside. I don't trust them—they know too much.

Really, Olivia says. It's an ongoing issue?

A judge has to rule on it, I continue. Whether or not it's an act of God. The rats smirk.

Charlotte asks if we can raise rats and I tell her sure and Olivia rolls her eyes and pulls back out. There's another one like a mile from here, she says. Hopefully no one is committing acts of God in there. By the time she gets us to the other location Charlotte and I have named all our rats—Ryan, Ridley, Rhea, Ronda, Ruby—and Olivia lets us know she thinks all the rats should actually be named Rebecca.

That would get confusing, I tell her, and she asks what I mean and I tell her I'd never know if I was talking to my army or to myself. She tells us to get our asses behind the cart. Charlotte whispers, Olivia gets moody when she's hungry, and I nod and Olivia says, I saw that, and then we're in the produce section looking at asparagus. The night does that: it moves fast. I'm feeling good. We're not in the place I work. I'm other, here. I'm customer.

The air-conditioning feels cold enough I think I've been folded into the freezer but the prices bring me back to the present just enough. A list, handwritten by Olivia herself, I assume, leads us. She gets good shit. Small, expensive cheeses. Pre-sliced cantaloupe. Prosciutto even though Charlotte tells her I don't eat meat. Remember, she says, and Olivia says, More for me then. She gets a bottle of olive oil that doesn't have a price tag but I know is a cool thirty bucks.

From the bulk selection, I select pine nuts (thirty-eight dollars per pound), dried apricots (eight dollars per pound), and dried thyme (six dollars per pound). Tall rats masturbate in front of the dehydrated soy curls and I don't know how to unsee it. I'm rolling the prices around in my head, trying to figure out how to convince Olivia to pick the cheaper shit. If there's one thing I understand, it's the power of a substitution.

We find Olivia at the raw cheeses after a semi-successful attempt of hooking up in the family bathroom. I got Charlotte braless on the changing table and we were going in on her soreness. Did she need to pump? It had been too long. We'd been out way too long. She couldn't keep doing this to herself. I don't know what she was seeing but I watched seagulls take flight from her nipples—they told me something about staying scrappy, about mothering as survival, and I smothered them in my throat when I swallowed each breast whole.

You need to love yourself, I told her. You need to drain when you're full. She was so into it she teared up. I rotated her nipples in and out of my mouth while she rubbed her clitoris. I asked if she liked being fisted. Fisting was something I could never quite bring myself to initiate with my wife, as I found it unbearably violent in its intimacy.

Charlotte hesitated then said she'd never done it but would once her nipples bled. I sucked both her breasts as far into my throat as I could—I was coughing and the seagulls had their wings out wide and proud, and Charlotte was bearing down, her hands keeping my shoulders in place—when knocks interrupted us.

Sorry, a woman said when I exited. My little guy had an explosion. When Charlotte squeaked out, she gave us both a dirty look and we fled in our giggles. I stay like that—goofy, light, irritating—until we reach the register. I don't recognize her right away but it's the bakery manager I interviewed with running this checkout station.

Somewhere in my brain, I knew this was a possibility; our company lets workers switch shifts across stores. People don't do it a lot but I curse myself for not thinking about the odds of it happening here.

I think that one will go faster, I say, nodding to the register next to ours. There's no way it will, of course; there are two toddlers pushing each other in the carriage. A woman is speaking quietly and quickly into her cell phone. There's a whole lot of canned pumpkin and applesauce waiting to be scanned.

This is ten items or less, Olivia says. And we're at ten.

Sometimes it gets tricky, I push. If the cashier is new, they'll be slower. I'm not letting myself look at the cashier directly; the noises coming from her sound like squeaks and I feel a frantic movement, like she's on the outskirts of a spinning tire.

You left the oven to preheat, Liv, Charlotte says. Didn't you?

I'm not moving, she says, and Charlotte and I look at each other and laugh.

At the register, I'm still laughing. I'm acting like I've never seen this woman in my life. Like I've never been in this store. Like I've never bought a grocery. Like I don't need food to survive. The woman is unfamiliar to me; she is a short and scrawny mouse. I expected her to be brown or gray but she's sallow and pale. I think I look like her scanning food; disinterested, soul-empty, weak. The manager ignores me until it's time to read the total and then she asks if I have my card with me. When she speaks, I see her rat fangs.

Oh, I say, not laughing anymore. That's like, so nice of you to ask, but I don't even know where it is.

Olivia says, I already entered my phone number and Charlotte says, Hmm?

I say: Nothing! I think I am going to faint.

Olivia says, I already entered my phone number. She has both her eyebrows up.

The manager looks at me and I feel the whole store has stopped. I will her not to correct Olivia. She's asking about my employee card, not a rewards membership, a 20 percent discount, but I can't think of how to explain it all to them.

We're good, Olivia says. Or whatever. She pays using her iPhone while Charlotte puts her face into my neck and kisses me with her tongue. I try my best to leave my body.

I'm really sorry, the manager says as she hands Olivia the receipt she said she didn't want. I mean, I'm sorry things didn't work out. I know she's referring to the job I didn't get but I react by giving her a sympathetic smile and telling her, Me too. Anything to avoid asking Olivia if she felt claws instead of nails. Olivia has a Mercury-ruled rising, I think, remembering Charlotte's character study from a few hours prior; she'd notice if our cashier was a mouse. I throw in a wink and she laughs then shakes her head. I'll let her think I'm crazy if it means Charlotte gets distracted by jealousy.

I think I am going to pass out from the stress and the drugs but we're back in the car and laughing again. Charlotte is telling her friend all about our first meeting; she calls it a first date, date, date, date, and I'm spinning in the back, but she's holding both my hands in her lap, and Olivia is going mm-hmm over and over and when Charlotte describes the waiter tripping, Olivia doesn't laugh. She doesn't even smile.

When we get inside, she says, I'll need one of you to chop and the other to peel. I ask what she's going to do, not meaning it to come out like a challenge but of course, it does. She looks over her shoulder to parallel park but stares right at me. I'm going to stop you from burning down my house, she says, looking around as though for an arsonist.

Olivia has everything. She has a blender and a chopper and a spinner. I open the oven once it's preheated and there are no spots on the bottom. No burned bits left from frozen pizzas on the racks. When the women have turned away from me, I reach into the oven and tiptoe my fingers against the hot bottom. There's nothing but stainless steel and then there's a spider trying to save herself. She's scurrying up my palm and then she's in my mouth.

Wow, I say. Your home is immaculate.

My cleaning lady is my best investment, Olivia says, and I mold her eye sockets into earrings. She goes into her budget, which Charlotte warned might happen; she receives a grant for eight thousand per cycle from the city, a separate grant for five thousand per semester from a local institution I haven't heard of, and she has some winnings from Europe-based contests. She maintains a close spreadsheet, or else how will she manage her spending? Her anxiety is all perception based; she would never lose this home.

These numbers confirm my suspicion: these girls have really rich parents.

Tell me what you'd do together if I wasn't here, I say (I swear I feel a phantom swallow in my throat and the salt of her tears between my teeth). Watch reality television? I feel combative, aggressive; I want to assert myself—*you're a nepo baby faux artist*—but I have no standing here. I'm self-sabotaging, as usual; instead of impressing Olivia, I'm picking fights with her. And I'm terrified she sees how fucked-up I am, thinks I'm a lightweight or an addict or junk. That self-awareness shines gold light through the grout lines of her backsplash: *I'm just like them.*

Charlotte says they'd probably be watching the Food Network and Olivia says they'd be dead and Charlotte elbows her in the side and they snicker. I wait. Charlotte says Olivia would probably be correcting the choices of contestants and Olivia says, What, because I'm so critical, and Charlotte says, Well yeah, and Olivia says, Oh, is that why you haven't shown me a spider in a while, and I say: Spider?

It's nothing, Charlotte says. I don't tell her there are webs in her eyelashes.

They're her little clay shrines, Olivia says. To Louise.

They're not *to* anyone, Charlotte corrects. They're . . . an homage.

I try to make my face placid but I'm rolling the word *homage* around in my mouth; I only vaguely know what it means, and I don't trust myself to repeat it correctly.

I ask why she's ashamed. I'm thinking: Those webs aren't real, those webs aren't real. The worst part of them being real, I think, is not that Charlotte could be hurt by them but that I hadn't paid enough attention to notice. I would have never let a web grow on my wife. The question shakes me in its simplicity: Am I fair to Charlotte? Of course I'm not. Why is she in this life with me, I think. I wonder if the spider knows.

Charlotte says: They're just a hobby.

Don't feel bad, Olivia says to me. Char makes all of this art that's like, miniatures of a famous dead woman's art. Those sculptures? Charlotte makes them teeny tiny and hides them in a shrine in her closet with candles and—

Dude, Charlotte says.

No, okay, there's not a shrine, Olivia says. But it's clearly *in conversation*, you know? Charlotte doesn't give her work the full push it deserves.

Do you know what Claymation is? Charlotte says to me and I feel stuck in space, back to watching old cartoons on video tape, stomach down on the rug of someone's family's living room. These aren't the memories I'm supposed to be having, these aren't the connections these girls want to be making. I shake my head no and they shake their heads no too. She tells me I do and I say, Like *Gumby*, and they say, Yeah. They're like clay models of real art, Charlotte says finally.

I bet your spiders are really good, I reply—or think I do; my voice feels distant, as though I'm channeling a god. I'm feeling more confident now that they're destabilizing and bickering; it's all jokes, but the tension could turn any second. I like watching people fight because it teaches me how to hurt others just as much as myself. And the webs are gone.

They're stupid, Charlotte says. I mean, it's stupid.

You're not stupid, Olivia and I say. We don't look away from Charlotte. Her chin is on her lap but there's nothing coming out of the tunnel of her mouth. I try to connect to Olivia with telepathy—not unimpressive, I reason—and ask: Are you seeing what I'm seeing? But if she is, she doesn't respond.

Your whole life would be different, Olivia says. If you respected yourself at all.

Damn, I say. Shit. I regret cursing immediately as I'm afraid of reading as uncouth or gauche, though I am both of those things. The cut in Olivia's voice surprises me; I want to drop inside her head and know what she knows about Charlotte. I wonder if I'm about to be kicked out—I must be among the decisions Charlotte makes because she doesn't respect herself, as I can't imagine Olivia would be as disgusted by anything as she would be by sex, otherwise they'd just be together. Or whatever it is we're doing, but my brain protects me from that train of thought by shimmying a rat tail around the recycling bin.

Excuse me . . . I say weakly. There's no way Olivia has a rat, right? She has a cleaner! I feel sick, like we're back in the black hole of Olivia's car but there's a darker darkness, a deeper one. I'm afraid the rats have come under the direction of God's will. Olivia shushes me and I realize the conversation has moved on without me; they don't seem to see the rat tail.

I'm the one who isn't a real artist, Olivia says after a time. I'm hardly producing. No one answers. I leave my body again. We all cool down thanks to some wine. We're all eating. Me more than the other two. We play cards and I lose.

Hey, Olivia says when Charlotte's in the bathroom. We can hear her pissing from our place in the hallway but I don't know where else to put on my shoes because I can't feel my legs and I don't trust myself to take a step. I didn't get your number. I nearly tell her she didn't ask but I just recite the digits. I almost always share it over text and I let that out and she laughs.

Sure, she says. Yeah. Then she tells me numbers and I say that isn't your full number, is it? And she tells me that's how much I owe.

For both you and Char, she says. All her teeth are where her eyes should be. That's okay, she adds, innocent-voiced. Isn't it?

Of course, I say, still not fully understanding. Totally.

I just assumed given your arrangement, she says. But I can totally Venmo her separately.

The account is one I share with Rebecca; we made it around the time we made our first checking account together so we could deposit our paychecks into the same place with our apps. The profile photo is from us on our wedding day; for the first time, I find myself wondering if maybe we could be taken as sisters or friends, something other than brides. The Rebeccas as another kind of joke. Rats are eating my eyes and my life with my wife is clear as ever.

No, no, I say. In fact, since you hosted, just give me the full bill.

Really, she says. Hosting is no trouble.

No, I say. I know. But really, let me do this.

She looks at me long and then says, Okay. A few blocks down the road, I block her everywhere.

18

CHARLOTTE WALKS RIGHT INTO THE PLACE RE-
becca's house-sitting. It's empty and she is impressed by
Rebecca's ability to find such a nice place to host her and
she hopes it involved some strenuous effort, like stealing
the key from the friend of a brother of a manager at the
market. She wants to imagine women finding her solutions, not merely folding her into their life.

To her chagrin, she is also feeling a lot of guilt. Enough
so that she texted Rebecca minutes after her shift, minutes before entering the house alone, started saying she
was really sorry and she had something important to
tell her and could they meet up at the house after work?
She wants to meet at a location Rebecca won't be able to
avoid or escape; she needs the house-sitting money, which
Charlotte isn't supposed to know, but she *does* know, and
how can she resist using her resources to her advantage?

She reminds herself a general would never doubt their ambitions.

Plus, she's been trying her best to be good. She'd stopped by the house the day after the dinner but she stayed in Olivia's passenger seat; the pair were en route to buy an elderberry syrup from the market, which the internet assured Charlotte would help with Rebecca's comedown. The brownie wasn't weed, as her studio mate confessed over voicemail hours after Rebecca's trip, but shrooms. And Charlotte found herself feeling fulfilled by mothering Rebecca, though she could not be certain if it was the nurturing she enjoyed or simply wearing her belly for an extended period.

Charlotte didn't think the trip seemed all that bad for it being unexpected, but that was before Rebecca started puking and crying at her house-sitting spot. She told Olivia about the caretaking immediately, because she wanted to be celebrated—look what a good, selfless person I am—and Olivia put her pride parade to an immediate end. Don't tell me you're hanging out with people who do psychedelics now, are you? I thought our limit was Molly?

She doesn't *do* anything, Charlotte explained. It's a martyrdom complex. Guilt and self-flagellation, the whole Catholic lot of it. She needs to loosen up.

But you *told her* what you had given her, Olivia said, strained, a mother leading a child in a divorce hearing, and Charlotte gave her a look.

You're not making good decisions, Olivia continued. You're acting like you don't have a future.

What do you mean?

Reckless risk-taking, Olivia said. Impulsive . . .

Attention-seeking, Charlotte interrupted. She was feeling angry, tied to a corner, and she looked pointedly at Olivia's thin wrists, peeking out from rolled sleeves. When was the last time she'd seen Olivia eat? Or mention food? She can't think of when, but she hasn't been keeping track.

It's beyond that, Olivia said. It scares me.

Maybe you're projecting, Charlotte said.

Why wouldn't *I* have a future, Olivia said coolly, sitting up straighter, and Charlotte reversed, said she hadn't meant it that way, how could Liv be so self-involved? I meant *you* were thinking *I* don't have a future.

Why wouldn't you have a future, Olivia said. What would draw me to that conclusion?

Projection, Charlotte said, causing Olivia to cover her own ears and scream.

Whatever myths she spun, it was enough to get Olivia into her car—ninety-seven degrees, Charlotte wasn't going to walk anywhere, and she wanted to go out without putting a bra on under her tank top, which meant she couldn't take an Uber because she didn't want to be seen by a man in such tight quarters. Even better to Charlotte, so delicious she hardly lets herself process it, is her story was so good, so overwhelmingly rich, Olivia didn't even make fun of her for wearing her belly out. She hardly snarked at all, just moved her big eyes around and insisted they were making air-conditioning colder, everywhere she goes she needs a fucking sweater.

The house alarm doesn't go off because someone—Rebecca, she assumes—must have left it unlocked. Briefly it occurs to Charlotte she could be walking into an armed robbery and she might be taken hostage and a special team might come save her and her unborn child, but she makes it to the kitchen without fanfare. She wonders how much these people are paying Rebecca and if she's supposed to have guests over and if Rebecca has brought her wife over yet. She glances at her phone and sees Olivia has re-sent her reminder to pay her for the groceries; *Your "partner" bolted talk about disorganized attachment style lol remember.* Charlotte sends a laughing emoji and Olivia says *do you think we should both start going to therapy* and *actually being honest LOL should I send you some profiles.*

Charlotte ignores the last text, approves the money request, eats an organic graham cracker—not stale, somehow, she notes—and thinks she would rather go into debt than ask someone to pay her back. A sickness finds a home in her stomach—why do I need to pay people to be nice to me? Why do I think I need to buy companionship? Because you're a bad person, she thinks. Because you're weird and lonely and you try too hard and you're a big lesbian with a weird fetish.

Charlotte fits three graham crackers into her cheeks and chews with her mouth open. Anyway, she says out loud to no one.

Her Rebecca has texted her: it's a picture of Bea sleeping against her chest. *My other favorite little spoon,* she's written. Self-hate seizes up in Charlotte. She could be sleeping in bed with them. Squeezed up against the wall, uncomfortable and moody about Bea's smell, but secretly, she'd be happy. Still, their relationship would have issues. Things for Charlotte to ruminate over with Olivia. The part where her girlfriend is trying to raise a baby with her ex-wife, Charlotte thinks sullenly. The part where her Rebecca isn't even her girlfriend—she's Charlotte's sugar baby.

Okay, Charlotte announces, standing. I'm changing my thoughts. She licks her finger and squats to pick up some fallen crumbs. It takes a few tries but the cracker bits stick; she sucks her finger until it hurts.

From the living room, Charlotte watches people walk by the house. She wonders when Rebecca was planning to arrive; if she's hoping they'll finally have sex full-out, she might want time to set up. She imagines a folding table and stirrups. Charlotte rolls her eyes at herself; she would ruin her own surprise by being early. She takes off her belly and tucks herself beneath a throw blanket in just her underwear; it's hot outside, but the central air feels so cold. She closes her eyes and imagines white balloons with pink and lilac ribbons. A box of three or four dark chocolates. Maybe Charlotte would have arrived to a hot bath filled with smelling salts. Lavender, she thinks. She smells it.

Charlotte rubs herself through her underwear and dreams. Both Rebeccas love her. They ravish her. The Rebeccas suck on her breasts together. Charlotte's dream self holds their heads in place and rubs their hair as they rotate her nipples in and out of their teeth. Her stomach is enormous, so they aren't entirely comfortable, but they don't complain. They love her stretched skin and its long stripes. And then the dream changes. The Rebeccas hear noises from the door; an intruder, they think. Charlotte tells them it's fine, to keep sucking, it's nothing, and at first, they listen. Charlotte feels that they're obeying her. Her dream self is worried, though—it did sound like someone trying to break in. But why? They're just having sex in a cloud. But the noise continues. Charlotte feels frustrated—can't she have one thing? The Rebeccas notice something is amiss, too; they keep making faces at each other, communicating without her, even though her nipples are in their throats. Charlotte closes their eyes.

Charlotte's dream self comes around when the Rebeccas hold a mirror up to her vulva. Oh, she says. Shit. The noises aren't from her giving birth, not exactly, but rather from a child exiting her. The baby has the dexterity of a toddler. The three women watch the baby rotate between smoking a joint and sucking a vape. Smooth, she thinks, then passes out when the baby wiggles its feet out; something about the toes on her vaginal canal is too much. She wakes to a noise with a panicked heart.

19

WE MAKE OUT FOR A WHILE BECAUSE I DON'T
know what else to do. My head feels clear for the first
time in days and I'm worrying about myself; what have
I been doing? What is wrong with me? With Charlotte
at my neck, I'm thinking: What the fuck what the fuck
what the fuck. I make her wait naked by the window
while I dig my harness out of my bag. I've already drawn
the curtain but her eyes are shut tight.

The floor is so cold, Charlotte calls. Can't we move to
the couch? I tell her she's not in a great position to make
demands and then lead her over. She bends her arm in
mine like we're walking into prom. Or what I imagine as
prom, anyway—I didn't go.

She sits on my lap on the couch. She looks down at
me for reassurance and makes what seems like a show of
touching her own nipples. I reach up and she pushes my

hand back down to her clitoris, where I had been rubbing her without realizing it. I resume and am surprised at how damp my hand already is, how much work I've been doing with my fingers.

We are saying the usual: *i'm so good she's so pretty isn't she i'm the best i'm better than she imagined i'm the whole world it's never been better can i believe how beautiful we are we look like a painting do you think anyone is looking in the window and feeling jealous do you think anyone is going to come from downstairs and watch do you think she'd look good pregnant do you think you're close* and I'm giving the usual *mmmhmmm totally so hot babe oh hell yeah duh obviously mhmmm.* Then I stop.

Charlotte, I say. This doesn't feel right. I feel unsteady; I'm surprised I don't lean into my instability to get really into the sex. Charlotte's face immediately drops, confirming my suspicion. She was performing, acting at least a little, being the cool chill girl, totally fine. Was she afraid of me? Was she trying to distract me? I can't make sense of it; I feel powerless to her. I watch her glance to the belly and wonder who she is missing.

Let's watch a movie, I suggest. I'm testing her and giving myself a way out, too; it's obvious what she's really after, but if she can't bring herself to say it, I'm not sure I have it in me to get us up to speed.

No, she says slowly. I want to have sex.

Mm, I say. I want to ask with whom but I can't remember if it's *who* or *whom* and I'm afraid of embarrassing myself so I just wait for her to continue.

With you, she says, giving me a look. Nothing is wrong. Her face is so forlorn I kiss her on the mouth.

Let's just try, I tell her. Without realizing it, I've begun to whisper.

Okay, she says, her voice very small.

I disentangle myself and pull a throw blanket around myself. I wiggle out of my harness because wearing it while standing gives me terrible dysphoria. I pull the blanket over my head. I hear Charlotte make little noises from the couch and ignore them. I don't know why I want to make this woman happy—or I do know why; I love fixing people, I love mess, I love an emotional roller coaster to focus on other than my own, and Charlotte has charmed me.

Come here, I tell her, still beneath the blanket. Let's figure this out.

I don't know what to do, Charlotte says. I've never gotten this far.

Well, I tell her. Your back must hurt, right? I rub her shoulders a little for emphasis and she curls her head into my wrists. And anyway, I don't think it's good for me to squish your belly.

Okay, she says quietly. I peek and she is beaming.

I lie down on the couch and coax her to sit on my face. Get up here, I tell her. I direct her to face forward so her belly covers my face. What a relief, I think. To be obscured.

I can't see your face, she says. Don't see me at all, I think. Good. I hold on to her calves and rub them. She hovers above me, and I notice she has goose bumps. I pull her down onto my mouth and her belly smacks me in the forehead. I don't mention it.

She shudders and I tap my finger against her inner thigh. She shakes and I pull the gusset of her underwear to the side and she stills. I breathe up into her vaginal canal so she shakes herself again.

Charlotte tells me her calves used to be big. I cried during ballet as a girl, she says. Then whined until my mother brought me to the doctor and was told I have hypotonia.

I hesitate, as this feels like the traps Rebecca set when it came to weight. What's that, I say eventually and Charlotte says, Low muscle tone. I tell her that her legs are beautiful, though I hadn't noticed her calves. In truth, they are closer together than one might expect while looking at the rest of her body. I see her clearly as a woman sweating in a dressing room, lamenting the tight ankle cut on jeans that fit the rest of her body. I wear my clothes too large to have had this problem in years, but the intimacy brings me back to seventh grade, fresh puberty, and the horrible indignity of stretching fabric around the sporadic bloat of my belly.

I take to her calves while she rubs her own breasts. I am not a hungry woman but one listening to my body's cues. I start my teeth at her right ankle, inch up, then turn to her left when she says my name. I fix my mouth as though I am going to gnaw into a large turkey leg, the sort that is popular at summer fairs and carnivals. Charlotte's calf would stand well on a stick. I press my teeth to her bone and she shakes as though I am at her clitoris. I wonder if she is touching herself and give her the dignity of not looking, as I can imagine no worse trespass than a woman monitoring my movements in the rare instances I enjoy my body.

My teeth don't leave marks but slight imprints. No one will see them within minutes, much less tomorrow morning. Still Charlotte reacts as though I have my fist up inside her, as though I am flexing my fingers and working my wrist in just the right way. I swivel my head between her knees on rotation. Some time passes. She pats her pubic mound and I look up, intending to tease her and make her spell it out—*what do you want say it tell me use your words guessing is for men*—and her belly obscures her, of course, and I am so warmed to her, I push her underwear to the side and don't speak.

I keep my mouth on her clitoris for a long time and suck in. This motion is my usual and as expected, it doesn't let me down. Charlotte shifts around on the couch and I move my head and upper body with her hips. My neck and shoulders are tight and compact. I imagine myself as focused as an acrobat. I tug my tongue in and out of her vaginal opening and use the bridge of my nose to grind against her clitoris and think of trapeze artists flipping in the space between my peaked shoulder blades. Rebecca is doing both the jumping and the catching.

I turn to my usual moves. I suck in my cheeks and grow spit at the roof of my mouth. I press my nose against Charlotte's clitoris then pull back and spit loudly. She makes a great noise and so I do it again and garner the same reaction. The third time, I spit but silently and her legs only twitch. From enjoyment or anticipation I can't tell and so I spit again, hardly any liquid but a lot of noise, and watch her revive her noise. My belly feels warm and happy. I appreciate her performance and the care she's putting into it—she is worried about pleasing me, and I understand this as an example of her loving or at least embracing me. I form my jaw into a bite and press my teeth against her inner thigh. She squirms and tenses and I pull my head back with my teeth still in a position to chew. Wow, she says, and I go into myself, try to remember the last time Rebecca and I had sex, but several sad times blur and I reorient myself to Charlotte's calves. Harder, she says from above. Please. I suction hard and I can tell her orgasm is real. She flinches when I breathe against her and I want to see if she'll tell me to stop or pretend it's still enjoyable. I suck her clitoris into my mouth and she jolts then squeaks an efforted noise.

Need a break, I say from beneath her.

No, she says, too quickly.

You're not sensitive, I say. You're sure? I breathe against her for effect. I'm thinking just say it just say it just say it. What I mean is: trust me enough to tell me the truth.

A little, she says. Then she apologizes and I hold her belly.

That's the patriarchy, I say eventually, thinking of how Rebecca might respond to a woman in this situation with a lecture. I tell her she can tell me next time, that she needn't suffer if she's too sensitive, and I try to get reassurances about her body and her needs and communication but she speaks over me and pledges that her post-orgasm sensitivity is the only thing she's been pretending about.

Can I come over tomorrow, Charlotte says.

Don't even go, I tell her, planning all the while how I'm going to leave.

20

THE LATE SUN HANGS LOW AND THE HEAT EASES. Charlotte's spider is visible from the sidewalk in the corner of a mostly empty green garden. One couple is standing too close to another statue and trying to take a selfie. A family is sitting in a circle on the grass and fussing at something in the center; Charlotte wonders if it's a baby, and she decides if she hears the baby cry, she's a good person, and if she doesn't, she's as self-absorbed as everyone thinks.

Beneath her spider, Charlotte closes her eyes and imagines a woman who looks like her sobbing on a big projected screen. She's eating popcorn and sitting in a nailed-down lawn chair and one of the Rebeccas— she can't tell which one, there isn't a face so much as a presence—remarks that, Jeez, she really looks like you. And Charlotte agrees a little bashfully. She commits this scene not just to memory but to soul. *So glad I got that off my chest,* she tells herself to think in the future, an epiphany orchestrated in advance: *Think about summer with the Rebeccas. So glad I've healed.*

I don't know who I am, she tells the spider. Her voice is small and weak. I only know what I want.

What do you want, the spider asks. Charlotte's impulse is to revisit the app. She wants to relist herself and see what women reach out—anyone who glossed over her before, suddenly more self-knowing (or more desperate), who wants to try their chance? Newbies who don't know better. Women like Other Rebecca who have their own secrets and won't press her for the truth. Distract me, she's thinking. Take me away.

I don't know, she lies, and the spider waits. Charlotte and the spider stay like that for some time—ants graze on the sweat behind her knees and a couple bickers about the angle of a selfie just feet away. She's visible, she knows, and she wonders vaguely what might happen if a video of her went viral. Anyone could do this, she tells herself. Anyone could cross the little black rope. Charlotte thinks that would be a good-enough distraction from the downfall of her romantic life, if only through the fall.

What do I do with my anger, Charlotte says. She feels uneven, afraid of how close she came to being discovered.

Hold it, the spider says. Love it back.

Charlotte is repulsed by the simplicity of this advice. I want to maintain my desires, she says. I don't want to outgrow my wants.

You want to stay small, the spider asks.

Charlotte, for the first time in the statue's presence, feels ashamed. No, she says. I want to stay myself.

You want to stay trapped in your pain, the spider sings.

That's a choice, Charlotte says. It's a choice I can make.

You're a girl who doesn't feel seen. And you'll throw tantrums until you get the love you want in spite of your bad behavior.

That's why you exist, Charlotte says, though she knows she's being unfair to Louise; the artist's childhood pain—if the split marriage of parents is in itself a trauma, a concept she is uncomfortable articulating—is part of her work, but certainly not all. It feels like a concern of the privileged, which she still struggles to identify herself as part of.

I exist because of you, Olivia says. I'm your conscience.

I don't want to be conscious, Charlotte says and the spider giggles.

How did things go with Rebecca, Olivia says. The important thing you had to talk to her about?

Which Rebecca, Charlotte says.

You tell me, Olivia says, her voice rising. You tell me everything, in your own words. I want you to hear yourself.

What, Charlotte says. She sits up and feels cool black above her head; she hasn't touched it, won't, but there's a presence, a sense of being held. She realizes Olivia's on the dirt beside her. She watches her friend flick an ant off her calf; so Olivia, she thinks, never one to let small enemies win.

How did you find me, Charlotte says.

I came to bring you back to reality, Olivia says stiffly. I want *accountability*.

Charlotte wants to quip that Olivia has nothing to hold over her head—what has she done lately that she needs to be accountable for toward *Liv*?—but she feels a truth serum in her throat.

I need to feel other stuff, Charlotte says quietly. I don't know what to do with peace.

Your work, Olivia says, and Charlotte shakes her head.

I think I've used it up, she says. I need to live more.

Can you *think* more, Olivia says. Literally, can you slow down more? Reflect—

I'm going to run away, Charlotte says. I don't deserve you.

This version of you doesn't deserve a lot, Olivia says. But you don't get to act badly just because you are bad.

I'm not bad, Charlotte says. None of us are *totally* bad.

Tell that to your girlfriend, Olivia says. Isn't she the one who hates herself?

She trusts me, Charlotte says, not sure which of the Rebeccas she's referring to.

I trust you, Olivia says, and Charlotte rolls her eyes.

It's time to get you back to yourself, Olivia says. She instructs Charlotte to hold her hand, and though the intimacy humiliates the both of them, their hot wet palms meet. Their fingers don't lace comfortably; they aren't lovers, won't be, either, but they're familiar. Olivia drives one-handed and Charlotte knows where they're going.

She could resist, but she wants her friend's attention—she's never gotten into the dirt with her before, after all, and she doesn't know what pain she'll have to display for it to happen again.

I don't think I'm a real person, Charlotte says.

You're as real as me.

I'm a cartoon, Charlotte says. An animated ant.

Ants have two stomachs, Olivia says solemnly.

What's the extra for?

The other ants, Olivia says pointedly.

This feels like an intervention, Charlotte says.

That's because it is, Olivia replies. She softens her voice, back to childhood.

Yeah, Charlotte says, embarrassed. Sorry. She's resistant to the diagnosis that she's self-destructing, as it feels cinematic, and all of a sudden, this lens disgusts her. I'm just a normal person, she's thinking. I'm not weird.

Sometimes I envy you, she admits. Charlotte feels her friend's body tense; I've failed already, she thinks. I've said the wrong thing.

What do you mean, Olivia says.

You act on it, she says. I think it must feel good, in a way. She feels rejection from her friend but trusts the spider will keep her safe.

Olivia frowns. You're always acting, she says.

I just mean it's nice to be seen—

It's actually very limiting, Olivia says. It's actually very limiting to be stuck being yourself.

Charlotte regrets knowing—she was expecting more hijinks, less haunting. I don't want to be alone, Charlotte says. I don't want to give up anyone or anything because I'm never going to get it back.

You don't want people to leave, Olivia says slowly. So you build a web?

I push them away, Charlotte says glumly. I can't keep a woman if I try.

You've always been self-centered, Olivia says, and Charlotte gasps despite herself, and Olivia adds that she didn't used to be this selfish. You're not thinking about other people, Olivia says. It's like you're living the kooky daydreams we all have, and you're acting them out inside your actual life.

What are your daydreams like, Charlotte says. She can't believe she doesn't already know the answer to this—it's being a famous artist, isn't it?

I don't have energy to dream, Olivia says.

So how do you fall asleep, Charlotte says. She almost calls her friend dramatic. Who lacks energy when they don't even have a job?

I read menus, Olivia says. And watch mukbangs without the sound.

That would make me eat all night, Charlotte says.

You're really something, Olivia says, and Charlotte tells Olivia she's the best friend she's ever had in her whole life. She takes Olivia for granted, she knows. One of their few barriers is Olivia's refusal to allow Charlotte to live selfishly without reproach. The real barrier, Charlotte knows, is her own fault; Olivia knows too much of Charlotte's past and present and it feels like she knows her future, too. Charlotte is so mortified at being known, she pushes and tests and teases, wondering what could break her skinny sidekick.

You've always been a bad friend, Olivia says.

I'm your best friend, Charlotte says, though she can't remember the last time she helped Olivia with anything.

You need to stop lying so much, Olivia says quietly. It scares me. And because Charlotte does love Olivia, she doesn't ask her which lie she's talking about. She says she's sorry, and she holds her belly, and both get red-faced looks.

Sorry, Charlotte says, louder.

Shh, Olivia says. I heard you.

Charlotte, ever-trusting and eager for affirmation from people who will not give it to her, details what happened with Rebecca, the frenzied sex. She sees me, Charlotte says, she really sees me. And she doesn't ask questions, she doesn't make me explain anything. She just . . . She just figures it out for herself. Charlotte squeaks out that even now, she herself isn't sure if she wants to raise the baby with her Rebecca (maybe), if she wants to keep seeing only the other Rebecca (maybe), or if she wants her art to be her baby, Rebeccas be damned (maybe).

How do I learn from something I haven't lost, Charlotte says, and Olivia pinches her stomach. Charlotte winces instinctively.

You're fine, Olivia says. You're so dramatic.

It hurts, Charlotte says. You're too rough.

It's not even you, Olivia says. It's your damn shell.

Kiss it better, Charlotte says, and the spider lowers her mouth.

21

MY WIFE AND I GO TO OUR FIRST CLASS ON CHILD development together. It was just starting when we got settled in the back. I feel like I'm back in high school—a loser, a disappointment, lurking as far away from the speaker as possible. Next to my wife, though, I feel cool. Unusual. *Those lesbians.*

Couples sit in front of us, some holding hands, some rigid in effort to appear professional and therefore void of intimacy. Rebecca doesn't go for mine and I'm not brave enough to try. I need to stretch, walk around. Shake some anxiety out. When an administrator offers the room some coffee from a big steel canister, I'm the first to accept. I think she must be a mother or something like one.

The social worker lets us know the day's focus is on *acclimation*. No matter what circumstances foster children come out of, she explains, moving into a new home is always stressful. Trauma, she says, long, like the word contains a couple hundred vowels. *Trauma*. She says we'll go over common signs of regression, aggression, and stoicism. She repeats that children don't have the same mental capacity we do and so they don't always understand that their actions can hurt others or even, she says with a lower voice, hurt themselves. I don't think she's doing the best job at selling everyone on the concept of inviting these kids into our homes but I guess she wants to lean toward honesty. I look at her long and decide she's definitely still on good terms with both of her parents who are, as they are proud to share, happily in love after thirty years.

I drink my coffee in a few swallows. Perhaps it's the folding chairs, or the dark roast, but the space reminds me of going to meetings with my mother as well as with my wife. I wonder if Rebecca's thinking the same and don't dare to look at her. We're in rows instead of a circle but the atmosphere sits the same: eager, polite, full of shame. Everyone looks like they could leave this room and approach a feeling by eating most of a fruit pie. My mother treated me to dollar-menu ice cream cones when she left meetings happy and slept through dinner when she left feeling too many things. I was small enough for her to convince other members I could stand in the hallway or distract myself by sorting cleaning supplies and paper plates in the closet while adults shared trauma after trauma. I remember her telling concerned members that there was no way I'd ever remember tagging along, much less what I heard. I stare past the woman at the front of the room and orient myself to where I actually am: not the basement of a school or a church but a city office building. I climbed six flights of stairs to get here. I crossed rotating glass doors to enter. My wife is sober. This space is nothing familiar. What is familiar is how lonely I am.

People have a lot of questions about moving backward; fundamentally, they want to know how many of these kids revert back to toddler status within a few days of moving into their new place. How common is wetting the bed? Shitting their pants? What about acting out at school, people want to know. The social worker impresses me in her ability to deliver bad news with a structured smile. What, her face says, you're going to back out over a little bit of piss in a mattress? With every answer, she reminds us that these kids have nowhere else to go.

I drop out of listening and study the pamphlets. Bodily fluids don't unnerve me the way the illustrations do. Not piss or puke but bodies close close close. Smaller bodies wrapped up in bigger bodies. All faces wearing smiles like they've found an unmalleable home. I imagine myself heating up a microwavable meal and blowing on it to cool the steam. Showing up five minutes early to pick up a kid from soccer practice. Making sure their white sneakers haven't yellowed between seasons. The hugs and kisses, the couch cuddles, the swinging by the armpits, though, unsettle me. I reassure myself my wife would have no problem and then I remind myself my role is limited to the period before our divorce finalizes. I could hug a kid for a month, could blow kisses when a school bus rolls into motion. Nausea lifts in my stomach so I tell myself to pay attention to the lesson. Under my breath, I whisper that I hate myself.

Rebecca glances at me but doesn't say anything. A few seconds later, she holds my hand beneath my desk. High school me would love this, I think. If she understood only the good parts.

An older couple in the front row has a list of questions. They probably wrote them down while at the dining table the night before; this couple, I can tell, has a big enough home to actually have a dining room separate from the kitchen. And what about drugs, the man wants to know, one hand still up in the air. What do we do if the kid comes home with a baggie in their lunchbox or we find rolling paper shoved in their dirty socks.

When the social worker tells him we'll cover intervention opportunities in a separate session, the man interrupts her transition back to bed-wetting and insists it's just a quick answer. Do we just call and they go to, what, do they go to juvie? Is that what they call it these days? Instead of telling him he should leave, or that he's not meant to foster, or that he should not have any sort of a child, or that these kids are not in-and-out options, aren't returnable in the way he is implying, the social worker pitches her voice and repeats that we will cover older children in a separate lesson. Then she passes out a worksheet on questions to ask a child's doctor to rule out chronic bladder problems.

And if they're nonverbal, someone seated in the front

row asks. If we can't figure out what they're wanting? I understand what's latent in her question: How can we be sure we're loving right? But I swallow my reaction, afraid of the vulnerability.

The two-option trick, my wife says. She doesn't raise her hand.

Go on, the social worker says. This language doesn't come from our session material and our leader looks curious—we all do.

My wife makes two fists. She's wearing her wedding ring. First you ask if they want to stay or go, she begins. Have them point or touch your hand. Then you put them back behind you—she demonstrates this for the room—while you think of your next question. If they want to go, give them two more options: Outside for air or the car for a drive? And then keep going until they start to open up.

Very intuitive, the social worker says. I'm wondering if she's guessing, like I am, that my wife picked up this emotional-regulation skill in her meetings. The social worker tells us all to write it down and I do. Then she taps the corner of my notebook and tells me I'm lucky to have a partner who values nonthreatening communication. I don't mention the self-harm threats that were once a regular part of our dialogue—hers or mine.

The whole world opens up, she says. When you're not operating from fight-or-flight. When she turns her back, my wife and I share a satisfied look: we're back in the world as a couple, perceived as a couple, and our love feels again both safe and exciting. Charlotte texts her address, and I tell my wife the notification is a reminder from Planned Parenthood for my pap.

Good, she says. I can't do this without you. What I hear is: I love you. What I do is: laugh, then run.

22

OLIVIA ORDERS ONE BANANA NUT OAT WAFFLE, no syrup, no butter, no whipped cream. Shaved almonds, yes. Cinnamon dust, yes. The second dish is one hash-brown cooked in the rough shape of a heart. Charlotte wonders if it's not Valentine's Day already, if her life hasn't skipped forward, if she hasn't missed an expected delivery date and been found out by all the people who've made her feel special. Motherhood looms like a punishment; did she think she could get all that adoration without the sacrifice?

Charlotte is sure the Rebeccas' foster placement, if it comes to fruition, would end her involvement in both of their lives. They'd still appreciate her money, if not out-right continue to need it, but her actual presence would be too much; neither Rebecca would have the energy for sex or talking or fighting in the fun ways. And what would her belly be if not a reminder of the real child they're leaving to be with.

And for you, the waiter says. Charlotte is relieved to see his clean hands and short fingernails; her mother taught her to always look at worker hygiene, kitchen staff or not. It sends a message, Charlotte hears, not in her mother's voice but her own.

She's having a hard time, Olivia says. Girl drama. The waiter mimes sadness, an exaggerated hand to the heart, and tells Charlotte he's delighted to support a local sapphic in her heartbreak. Charlotte puts a hand to her chest and smiles broadly; she hopes she is beaming, but she knows a light is missing, and she wants to blame it on the Rebeccas, but really, it's her own fault for being at the diner. Olivia could have eaten other places. Other gay waiters could have fawned. But her Rebecca's AA group comes only to this diner, on only this night. Her Rebecca says it's exclusive to this specific fellowship and this specific meeting, which Charlotte respects but finds infuriating.

What's your best heartache food, Olivia says. What do the girls cry into?

Charlotte looks beyond her friend and the waiter as they modify burgers (house-made lentil patty instead of pea protein), sauces (Dijon in place of aioli), and fries (sweet potato over parmesan truffle). Charlotte learns she's to receive modified versions of The Little Chabang (pseudo Happy Meal including a vegan double cheeseburger, fries, roasted brussels sprouts, and a small matcha), Cheesy Delights (deep-fried cheese with a guava dipping sauce), and one slice of vegan chocolate cheese-cake pie. Extra hazelnuts on top. Charlotte loves letting Olivia take control because it means she can look for her Rebecca.

Maybe the group has a standing reservation, which would explain why they need to cap the number of people who come. Her Rebecca is there, chatting at the host stand in a sundress and cardigan and flats, and Charlotte imagines sending her money with a coffee emoji. *My treat*, she could write. The other people mostly look as Charlotte expected but also better, which shames her. There are artists, or at least people who are okay with being read as such. A few gays who couldn't hide if they tried. Mostly people sweating in suits. The sort of people Charlotte watched her parents socialize with as a child. Could Rebecca be honest about herself in a room with people in suits? With anyone? Give me that vulnerability, Charlotte thinks. Just me.

Okay, give me the rundown, Olivia says. Charlotte can tell Olivia's feeling magnanimous and she herself wants the attention, but she's wary of it, too. What if Olivia gets upset and doesn't get a bite down?

Which of the Rebeccas are we waiting for, Olivia says. Or is it both?

It can only be one, Charlotte says. Guests aren't allowed.

Okay, Olivia says. Does she know we're here?

No, Charlotte says. Of course not.

Olivia nods. Charlotte waits. Olivia tells Charlotte to get one horrible shameful thing out of her head and onto the table so they can eat its spirit with dinner. It's about dominating our fears, she says. Charlotte has questions about this approach, but she can't see her Rebecca well from where they're seated, and the place is too popular to make it easy to switch tables, so she says she's been thinking a lot about the fantasy she has about being rushed home to be shaved. She'd be horny but too big to bend, she says, so she'd want to modify her body in ways she could control. So she'd wait until Rebecca—parallel Rebeccas, in parallel worlds—had just started an important and arduous task and then call repeatedly and ask for her to come by and help her shave down there. And the Rebeccas would hesitate; come on, they'd be thinking. Really? Is she really worth all this? Charlotte loves luxuriating in that suspension, the opportunity she gives people to abandon her tight world. Because of course they'd come. They'd massage her with a nice bar of unscented soap and use a clean razor and afterward they'd massage her hips and perineum.

With her mouth full of fried cheese, Olivia says, I hear you. Charlotte waits for more, and Olivia covers her mouth with a hand, continues to chew, and informs Charlotte she understands where she's coming from.

Everyone wants to be accepted bare ass, she says. Anyway, I didn't think you still shaved. Do you think that's why you're in a juvenile-in-love flight-or-fight response?

I don't know, Charlotte says. Sugaring hasn't worked well for me.

Do you want the referral code for my laser removal place?

Are you serious, Charlotte says.

Duh, Olivia says. My mom has a budding pyramid scheme going with getting this waxist's number out. But she's actually really nice. She's good about focusing on my body without focusing on my body, you know what I mean?

Totally, Charlotte says. The additional dishes arrive and the waiters slide over another small table because they've ordered enough for four people and this is not the sort of establishment where space is cheap. Olivia is the happiest girl Charlotte has ever seen, as she dances her hands over the food in front of her. When the workers are done fussing, Olivia switches her waffle for Charlotte's double cheeseburger without speaking.

I'm proud of you, Charlotte blurts, then excuses herself to the bathroom so she can look for her Rebecca and check up on the other Rebecca in peace. She also goes because she loves Olivia, and she knows it's a kind of gift to let her be herself.

Finding the bathroom is its own kind of hero's journey. There's a room for families, which Charlotte would use if not for the actual family with actual children waiting outside—no one would bat an eye if she had her belly—and then there is a room with urinals. Nothing is in a row, and people are everywhere.

Excuse me, she says to the waiter. Do you have a single-person bathroom?

What, he says.

A single-person bathroom, she repeats. Like just a regular bathroom?

For one person, he says. A regular bathroom?

Charlotte thinks she's about to faint. How is her friend betraying her? Did she dream his fawning over her? I spotted my ex here with another woman, she says evenly. And I just need a space to fall apart.

I understand, he says.

You do, she says.

My sister, she has an eating disorder too, he says. It's like, totally consuming her life.

It is, Charlotte says.

Yeah, like. She's older than me, and even though I work at like, a shitty restaurant—no offense, you know what I mean—I'm still more of an adult because I manage to, I don't know, put my rent on auto-pay and actually clean my dishes and not piss off my roommates. But she's like, at home, thinking about food. You know what I mean?

Totally, Charlotte says. Her relief sickens her; this man's sister is really sick, and Olivia is sick too, but she isn't like, wasting her life away. She's an artist! An artist with a grant. An artist with opinions.

See, Olivia says when Charlotte returns to the table. You can still get attention from strangers without . . . she drops her eyes to Charlotte's torso.

You're the best, Charlotte says, because she wants Olivia to stay happy enough to eat. Always looking out for me. Charlotte stays in this moment as long as she can; Olivia, surrounded by food, being a good girl, eating her fill. Olivia is dearest to her of all people; she is, Charlotte knows, responsible for Charlotte's entire life. It would have been easy for Charlotte to date men, not because she enjoyed it, or because she wanted to, but because the role was so clearly defined for her, one she could understand intellectually, if not emotionally. Olivia's lesbianism showed Charlotte a happiness that couldn't be denied. If Olivia wasn't quite so Olivia, maybe Charlotte would be closeted and masturbating to erotic short stories about flirtatious dykes and shy bisexuals. And maybe she wouldn't catch the women she's seeing with one another and want to die, either.

The Rebeccas are sharing a plate inside the diner. Her Rebecca is sitting down and Other Rebecca is standing behind her; she doesn't have her own seat. She came late, Charlotte thinks. She wasn't on the reservation. Does she go to meetings now too? As a spouse? A friend? Charlotte wonders if the other Rebecca pretends to be an addict in order to go; she's thought about doing that, but something about it feels off; she can't distract herself by diving into other people's secrets if she wants real relief from her own. Charlotte watches Other Rebecca eat bread from a basket in the center of the table. There's a lot of bread and butter and a few appetizers arranged between the eight or ten people seated at the table. Only her Rebecca has an extra person behind them. Everyone at the table has a water glass.

Charlotte puts her hands on her stomach: bloated from dinner, but not enough to be in pain or, more valuably, to appear pregnant. Charlotte wants to condense the restaurant into a splinter and stomp it down into the ground.

I had no way of knowing she'd be here, Olivia says. Her voice enters Charlotte's head like a rhythm, something she comprehends but cannot define. Char, you're hearing me, right? You can't make meaning out of this, running into those women.

Do you think they've seen us, Charlotte says. Did you notice anyone looking?

Running into your ladies was a joke because I didn't think she'd actually be *that* shitty, Olivia continues. Charlotte registers, vaguely, that Olivia has stopped eating. Her fingers shine with butter. It was outrageous, Olivia continues. And that's why it's funny—

I feel flooded, Charlotte says stiffly. Emotionally overwhelmed. Can we go outside?

Inside the car, Charlotte screams like she's been told to push and Olivia moves her hands like a conductor.

23

CHARLOTTE INVITES ME TO A COUPLES MASSAGE about forty-five minutes before the appointment time. I cannot miss work so last minute without a replacement or doctor's note. I need a quick Heads or Tails—the birds, I decide, can help. If the pigeons land before they disappear into the horizon, I go to the massage. If they land where I can see them, I tell her no and go to work. Either way, I'm choosing the same fate.

Late night, Charlotte texts. *Tired???*

I'm thinking: Coincidence. It was a late night, but it always is; I stay up as late as I can to regain the control I don't feel when I'm up and around other people. I was at my wife's, watching her and the dog sleep.

Exhausted, I reply. *Rejuvenated at the thought of you.*

In response, she sends the address. Google shows me

a bunch of dollar signs and I imagine robbing Olivia and selling all her dehumidifiers and water filters.

See you inside, she adds.

I'm in my work uniform and ready to cover the latest shift I took in exchange for having the big house to myself. I stare at my phone and weigh my options: if Charlotte is at a spa downtown, she's less likely to come into the store while I'm working the register, and that's a relief. I look up and the pigeons are out of sight. But where? I decide they're still flying, giving me permission to get some aches out of my blood.

On the other hand, I feel guilty about Rebecca and the ugly baby. We spent last night together. My wife and I, I mean. The baby, just metaphorically or figuratively, I don't know. I was watchful, attentive, she was sparkling. We were in our old way and on good behavior, trying to impress one another—see, I, too, am human enough to change. It was almost enough to make me tell Charlotte no, but seeing her feels entirely necessary. When else have I experienced a woman so fully herself, with no support from me?

I want reassurance that I can be the sort of woman Charlotte thinks I am, the sort of woman who is available for an impromptu spa day at a place so expensive it doesn't even list prices on its website. I can't afford one massage, much less two, and I've been worried about what I'll say if Charlotte calls my bluff and asks me to actually pay for something. Is it wrong of me to let her keep paying, what, because she's so ashamed, because she feels so unworthy, she feels she has to play both roles to keep me around?

I want to tell her I'm not worth it but I haven't felt so special since I met my wife and I am a weak person. I open my texts to let my coworker know I have to bail last minute, sorry, but I type then erase it. I intend to tell her I just forgot; I would be so mad if she did that to me, but I tell myself that's another life, another version of me—the me that doesn't get offered free alcohol and heated towels. The me that holds the door for customers. The me that no one sees.

The spa is located inside an enormous old hotel. I've never been inside but I've walked by the building on my way to the Mall. Straight couples take pictures outside during golden hour and unhoused folks sleep on the stairs at night. When I took a few overnight shifts at the market across town, I crossed this street to get home in the early hours of the morning. With Charlotte, on a busy Sunday afternoon, I can almost convince myself it never reeked of piss. Almost.

The hotel lobby is white and grand and marble. The doors are heavy. I feel like a criminal for noticing this and for thinking of how frustrating it would be to try and rush out of this place with one of those fancy robes shoved into your bag just to come upon these big thick doors. If Charlotte notices the amazement on my face, she doesn't mention it; she seems focused on getting us to the spa in time and walks a half step ahead of me. She knows to slow down each time a worker holds the door for her and I have to resist the urge to push the door myself.

At the spa, the receptionist says Charlotte's name

and my first name. Right, Charlotte says, quickly. Right. She nods at the waiting area and offers to get us waters, but she won't look at me. There's a pitcher with lemon slices and a pitcher with lime and a pitcher with a fruit I can't identify which means it's expensive. I nod toward that one and Charlotte is kind enough to inform me it's a ginger-lemongrass blend. Charlotte appears careful while balancing the glasses—they sound heavy, not plastic, impressing me—and I find myself missing her. Without thinking, I put my credit card on the desk.

For both of us, I say. Charlotte opens her mouth to protest, I guess, and her phone vibrates. She apologizes a few too many times while staring at the screen. She's hiding something, but what, I don't know. It occurs to me that my card is going to be declined. As the massage therapists lead us into the back, I reassure myself I can always pretend to discover a fraud alert blocking all transactions. I feel good about this plan.

The women talk at us and show us where we can strip down. There are robes and heated towels. We're offered three types of tea, sparkling and still water, and prosecco. Charlotte takes the wine and sniffs it—It makes me feel like a free woman, she says, laughing, and inspired by her confidence, I ask for a tea; my massage therapist doesn't hear me, immediately humiliating me, and I learn I pronounce *rooibos* wrong. As though offering an ointment, she tells me she'll bring it with a carafe of oat milk. I'm so embarrassed by her kindness I want to die so once the door is shut I tug up Charlotte's bra and pull her nipples into my mouth.

Oh, she says. Holy shit. My eyes are still open when

she covers her own mouth with her open palm and I go in at her areolas with my teeth. Her pants get caught around her thighs and when I step on the crotch to get them down to her ankles, she gasps. The part of me that doesn't feel uneducated and small and worthless feels very powerful. I don't go down on her, not really, but I do get on my knees and give her a few licks. There's rustling at the door and I tell her to lie face down on the bed and think of me the whole time she's being touched. By the time they give us the warning knock of reentry, I convince myself she sees almost no holes in my facade.

This self-delusion works well enough until the massage therapist puts a hot stone on just the right part of my shoulder and I rear up and hit. No one sees it coming; I'd been yessing and mm-hmming to all her explanations of what she would do and why and when. The stones feel almost too hot, but not unbearable. She's in a spot that scares me but it's not pinpointed enough for me to tell her Please not there or Maybe to the left or That area is too sensitive. When she inches around it I'm wishing I had been in tennis lessons or on a soccer team or had survived a crash; I'm sick enough to envy people with traumas that don't sound as shameful. I've barely told my wife I was molested as a kid by that creep uncle; there's no way I'm telling a stranger hired to touch my disgusting self.

I'm so, so sorry she says, but it's not her fault, and I tell her that. Everyone is staring. Charlotte is sitting up with her breasts uncovered and I notice her nipples are little rocks. I wonder if she's aroused at my fear or if her body understands it as anger or something else.

The woman working on me says she's so sorry so sorry so sorry so sorry and I tell her it's fine it's fine it's fine it's fine I don't know what happened. I want to pull her aside and level with her; I'm not one of those rich people you have to grovel with, I think. I'm not a traitor to my class. But I'm in Charlotte's world, and I'm paying, and the part of me that was raised to find creative solutions thinks I've stumbled into my next fix.

I cover my face and curl into myself. It's like I'm crying but I'm not; I've gradually lost the ability to cry while others are within earshot, as I was described as whiny and bratty and spoiled as a child. Sitting on the massage table, I am between spaces: I am the little girl reading the advice column of a magazine, learning that the way she's been touched by her aunt's latest boyfriend is inappropriate and wrong and a crime and needs to be reported to a trusted adult. I am also the woman who is broke. Performing trauma, performing grief, is easier when I tell myself I'm only an actress.

After much back-and-forth among the others, we continue the massages. The masseuse uses the lightest touch. No stones. No heat. She checks in with me even when I stop sniffling. When the bell chimes, the workers gather in the hallway to whisper and Charlotte fashions her sheet into a toga.

Rebecca, she says, and I cry for real. The workers knock and Charlotte hustles to the door. I hear murmurs of *so sorry* and *no problem* and *it's on the house*. Charlotte says something about cash in her wallet, she'll handle it when we're dressed.

I love you, she says to me. There's no air-conditioning in the room and I blame the outburst on that.

I feel really special, she continues. That you'd come here with me.

It was hard for me, I admit. I'm thinking of when Rebecca wanted to get a couples massage after our wedding and I did but I didn't relax. I stayed so tight it hurt. The masseuse, my wife later told me, targeted all the spots she injured playing club softball as a teenager, the wrists and knees and shoulders. My masseuse kept whispering, asking if I was alright, telling me I could speak up anytime, and I said, Mm-hmm, and tried my hardest to leave my body. I told Rebecca it was great and she loved me enough to never book us one again, Groupon deals be damned.

I felt safe with you, I tell Charlotte, and surprise myself with my honesty. When she kisses me, I see a terrible sadness. Oh, I think. She's my mirror. I pretend not to notice when she slips my credit card into my pocket. When she leaves cash for the tips on the desk, she doesn't count her twenties. I tell her I love her on the sidewalk outside and she tells me she feels a rainbow coming in the mist. She puts her mouth to my ear and I hug her waist and feel like we're in a movie and she tells me, really, not to pay for stuff.

I don't think that part of the dynamic works for me, she says. It might cheapen it.

AT MY WIFE'S, we sit side by side on the bed and hover around her laptop. She's been in bed with a headache all day and when we see our application has progressed, I go into fixer mode. I have questions—lots of questions. Does she want the overhead light off? Should I take Bea out? Can I get her some medication? Can she make an appointment?

I love being loved by you, she tells me. I feel like I'm in a cocoon.

We feel safe together, I say, thinking of Charlotte. It's been just hours since I was licking her labia in the spa.

I'm bidding for your attention, she says. You know that. She's right: I do know that. We cycled through a number of self-help relationship books before I left and the bid-for-attention concept stuck with us both—turn toward your partner instead of away, understand what they're really getting at when they prod or poke or push. I don't want to acknowledge Rebecca's attention because I don't want to lose it. I don't give it back enough, I think; I am just a lukewarm body.

I really appreciate how you show up for me, I say, textbook perfect. You've always done a good job of taking care of me.

When she beams and hugs me from behind, she presses her torso into my bruises. The pressure hurts and we both know my refusal to flinch is my way of admitting I still love her.

Charlotte

24

CHARLOTTE SETTLES INTO THE COMMUNAL STU-
dio with her phone on Do Not Disturb and an iced cap-
puccino sweating at her feet. These decisions are not mere
details. It's about mood, she knows. Atmosphere. Things
feel empty and good; her Rebecca is really, really mad at
her, as a result of Charlotte calling in the wee hours of the
morning and interrogating her about why she couldn't go
to the diner with her post–AA meetings. *Are you ashamed
of me?* She managed not to bring up recognizing her wife.
Rebecca told Charlotte she needs to go to therapy and
hung up. Charlotte sees herself putting this pain into art,
into being productive. She thinks about texting Olivia
a picture of her workspace and decides to wait until she
has something to show for herself.

While working on her senior project in undergrad,
Charlotte attempted a knockoff Louise. She entertained

visions of a pregnant spider birthing identical spiders that appeared dead or alive depending on the light. The impossibility consumed her focus—control the light? How? What does a dead spider look like versus a living one? She imagined a cluster of spider eggs smoking a blunt, the mother spider chiding the risk-taking of their youth. What does it look like when spiders greet the world? Charlotte couldn't bring herself to google it. She surprised herself by committing to the bit. She molded her spider and her babies (thirteen in total) out of alabaster, requiring a delicate resin. She worked hard but she couldn't look at her completed projects—the transparency of her creations humiliated her. She found her own technique amateur and desirous, the most embarrassing things to be. It was so like her, Charlotte knew, to choose a delicate, breakable foundation then resent it for its cracks, its simple vulnerability. During critiques she stared at the soapstone ant colony beside hers instead. Even at thirty-seven, years away from the studio, Charlotte prefers to stay in that moment, not to hear what comes next, not admit how mortified she'd been by her classmate's assessment. The spiders will get a better mark, she said. Really, Charlotte had said, breathy, stupid. Because it's expensive as fuck, the classmate continued. That won't matter, Charlotte had said. They're not supposed to consider that. Rich people will complain about anything, her classmate said. That's why people are so nice to them.

Charlotte shakes her head at the memory. Charlotte is frazzled by her Rebecca's tightened boundaries, bricks added to the moat, and feels she's losing control of the other Rebecca—her reaction to the massage made Charlotte feel good, because she likes excitement, but also bad, because she doesn't want to be responsible for anyone, including herself. Charlotte doesn't remember her Rebecca mentioning that her wife had been sexually abused; it makes her feel good to think maybe her wife doesn't even know. She shudders; she's thinking like an artist and the self-importance mortifies even her.

Hello, a voice says. Hello.

Charlotte snaps, What, and the woman steps before her. Dude, she says. Your phone's been going nuts. You don't hear it?

Charlotte does hear the beep but she hadn't realized it was coming from her device. She's never had anyone override the Do Not Disturb function; she wonders which of the Rebeccas is melting down, which has decided she cannot live without her. Pick one, she's thinking as she grabs at her phone. Know yourself. But their faces sit behind her eyes like baby birds in a nest.

In the end, it's only Olivia. Jesus, she says. Are you okay? The studio mate is lurking and Charlotte wants to shoo her. Focus, Charlotte wills herself. Focus. She hates the classmate, with her oversized linen and her dingy Louis Vuitton sneakers.

I need help, Olivia says. Her voice is very small.

Liv, she says. Where are you?

I don't know, Olivia says, her words slow and long like syrup. Out.

What do you mean you don't know, Charlotte snaps.

I hear people. Just ask someone where you are. Olivia doesn't speak. There's music and people, Charlotte continues. You're out with someone or you'd be home. Can you just send me your location?

I'm alone, Olivia says, and Charlotte feels afraid.

You're drinking on an empty stomach, Charlotte says. She's thinking: Don't be shrill, don't be shrill. Ask the bartender for water and order fries.

I don't want fries, Olivia says, though Charlotte knows she is lying.

Charlotte is ordinarily happy to give Olivia permission to eat, because it makes the both of them so happy, but Olivia's eating habits, especially when she's alone, have worried Charlotte from the start of their friendship, since she noticed Olivia counted carrots and dipped them in mustard during a trip to the movies. In that cool dark room, Olivia looked small, weak, ill; she looked like exactly the sort of woman Charlotte imagined a serial killer might go for, betting she wouldn't put up a fight. Charlotte paired a sense of superiority with her gluttony, her wanting, for years as an outlined shield between them; Olivia manufactured attention from people by hurting outwardly, and Charlotte manufactured attention by acting as a puppeteer. But if this is all about Olivia eating a dollar slice before going home, Charlotte isn't having it.

Send me your location and I'll handle the Uber request.

Olivia says nothing. Charlotte hears "Lucky" blasting in the background and men cheering. She names one gay bar, then another, and then Olivia squeaks out a Yeah, that one. Charlotte checks the bar's hours and informs her it's closing in thirty minutes. She repeats herself and Olivia says, Yes, I know. Charlotte clings to normality—Olivia managed to make a call, didn't she? She must still be standing. But her voice is at once thick and frantic, like her body can't keep up with her feelings. Charlotte smiles to feign a sense of control in the chance the artist is actively observing her, but she is afraid. She is very afraid. Charlotte checks her texts as a self-soothing measure and sees a request from Other Rebecca: *Lamaze*, she wrote. *Your place?*

When, she texts. This game sounds fun, distracting. She imagines pushing until the belly comes right off.

Olivia, she says into her phone. If I order you a car, will you get in it?

That's not what this is, Char, she says. That's not what we're doing. She speaks clearly, now, like a woman who has come to a decision.

Can you wait for me to come and get you? Charlotte doesn't want to go across town to get Olivia. She knows her hesitation makes her a bad person, but she believes Olivia coming to her would benefit everyone; Olivia can have an emotional moment in the back seat of a private ride she isn't paying for and Charlotte can get eaten out while pretending to give birth. Charlotte tells Olivia there are hot fries in the vending machine.

I'm good, Char, she says, suddenly warm. You're so sweet.

You're not good, Charlotte says.

I'm going out with some people, Char, she says. We're going back to someone's place to hang.

What people, Olivia? Charlotte feels herself getting very warm. She looks for the lurker and sees her leaning over an easel with large headphones. Do I call 911, she wants to ask this stranger. Do I call the bar? She doesn't know how to keep Olivia safe; can't she be sick in just the one way, not all of these variations? Charlotte tells herself to move her feet but she doesn't want to be the hero. She wants someone else to take over, someone smarter and better equipped. She wants Olivia, but Olivia is her mess.

She checks her messages and sees her Rebecca has texted her: *social worker comes tomorrow, send good wishes, love your support always :)* and Charlotte sends a heart. She wishes she could retract her heart and make her wait but her message appears as read almost immediately.

Got more gear—bassinet and little tub and colorful baby books, her Rebecca texts. *Couldn't do it without you love.*

Without my money, Charlotte corrects out loud. In her mind's eye, the bassinet crowds the already-microscopic apartment—what room for Charlotte is there? She sends a series of hearts and reminds herself that at least that enormous plant, the bird-of-paradise, is taking up space in the studio. Think of me always, she thinks. All she wants is dominance.

I'll see you soon, Char, Olivia says. Remember, don't stress if I don't answer.

Why wouldn't you answer, Charlotte says. What am I supposed to remember?

Olivia laughs. Did you not listen, she says. Or did I not speak?

You're scaring me, she whispers. Olivia doesn't respond but the voices behind her are louder, closer; they're talking about how many cars to request, firming up plans with everyone. The voices are all male and drunk. Charlotte tells Olivia not to get into anyone's car and to wait for the one she's sending. She checks the app; the ride's been approved, and the driver is on their way. They have a drop-off before the pickup.

Are you okay, the studio mate interrupts. You look stressed?

I'm fine, Charlotte says. Latent in her tone: mind yours.

It's cool, the girl says. That you're keeping up.

Thanks, Charlotte says. She wants to be the cool girl, unaffected.

I'm a little surprised, the studio mate continues. Where does Charlotte know her from? Does the memory go all the way back to braces and she's blocked it out? Charlotte sees this girl as her younger, scrawnier self—was she one of the girls who called Charlotte a slut all those years ago? Charlotte blinks until those visions go away.

What did you say, she asks the girl.

The fumes, she says. I'm surprised it's not bad for the baby.

Mind your business, Charlotte snaps, and the girl, for the first time, looks truly impressed. Charlotte feels powerful until she realizes Olivia is no longer on the line.

Rebecca

25

MY WIFE IS TELLING ME I'M THE MASTER BEHIND this miracle. I completed all my training hours and it's bumped us ahead in the system; I'm thinking, I did? I hadn't kept track. Thirty hours sounds like a lot to someone who is pained by living. Rebecca swears we're scheduled for a home visit with a social worker. Again and again, I ask Rebecca if she's sure; I don't want her to get excited over a misunderstanding. No, she replies. It's us.

Us, I cling to. Us, us, us.

Leaving Charlotte is easy. A good person would not feel this way but I have never claimed to be good. I see my future with Rebecca, with an ugly baby, and many other blessings: vegetarian breakfast sausages, alcohol-free IPAs, health insurance, awkward and unsatisfying Thanksgivings at her parents' place, mutual masturbation during sex. I will never tell her about Charlotte. I will never tell her about the app. If Charlotte lashes out, I will block her. If Charlotte points out I never bought her anything, I will call her selfish. In our real lives, as I am kissing Charlotte on the forehead and telling her to make sure she doesn't skip breakfast, I remain in my head, making a point to romanticize the moment to myself: I will never see her again and she could have been special to me.

The city installed portable air conditioners so we're all feeling good at the session. I sit in the back. My wife and I are going to have a baby. It might have been born addicted to drugs. It might have been living in a car. It might have a sibling we aren't getting. This is the only thought I worry about: Where are the others? A toddler could sleep in our bathtub, I decide. If there are two toddlers, well. We have that top shelf in the closet where we keep the clothes that fit. A baby could sleep in many places.

The old man gets called up for today's activity. The one who is obsessed with the idea of his foster bringing drugs into his house. I want to tell him they probably will; I did, after all, just a few joints and the occasional edible I got from a friend's boyfriend's cousin. These people always imagine the future as worse than it is, I think, watching him squirt some sanitizer into his hands at the front of the room. As he waves his hands (to get the evaporation going, he tells us, and no one but the social worker laughs) I decide he is the kind of man who has had a good life but is driven by anxiety. No, not driven. Controlled.

The social worker tells the man he is going to be himself and she is going to be the foster child. He agrees, looks around the room, and I imagine his wife gives him a smile. I'm in that kind of mood: generous, superior. The social worker speaks to him in a low voice; not a whisper, not that intimate, I decide, not quite like she gave me, but a little advice, sure. He nods, and surprises me by not asking any clarifying questions. We can all grow, can't we.

I'm leaving, the social worker says. Don't try to stop me.

I think, Oh, it's that kind of day. I expect the man to grab her and when he doesn't, I tell myself that must have been what they were communicating: No touching, no grabbing, no flipping her over his shoulder like a stunt double.

He tells her she is her own person but he would prefer her to stay, and I roll my eyes; Come on, man, I'm thinking. Express a little. She pleases me by getting louder, huffing, circling the front of the room. You're never going to see me again, she says.

Tell her you don't want that, I am thinking. Tell her you love her and you don't want her to go. But he repeats himself: She is free to go, he won't limit her, but he would like her to stay.

I don't care what you want, she says. I care about what I want.

I want what you want, I think. I want you to be happy. How can I make you happy?

It scares me when you threaten to leave, he says. Can we agree on a time to check in if you do decide to leave our home?

She's not going to check in, I think. She's going to disappear.

I don't even like you, she says. Don't you realize how unhappy I am?

My body is tight and I am present—too present. I want to go inside myself and I do, but it scares me: Rebecca is drinking on her medication again and her moods are bad. She is yelling and our neighbors are making noises in their homes, warning us to quiet down or they're going to call the police. When she's quiet, she makes threats against herself and I worry my crying will be the reason the cops show up. I chew socks to stifle myself and she reminds me I am pathetic. This part of my past is a nightmare but it's real and so I can't disappear it. I am always wondering if she loves me enough to stay alive or if she loves me so much she'll resent me for living.

That is hard to hear, the man tells the social worker. We don't want anyone in our family to be unhappy.

So make her happy, I think. I don't know what that looks like or what he should do. I understand, even, there is nothing he can do; it is not about any one action or purchase or promise. It is about making it clear he is going to do all the things that don't matter. He is going to try.

I wish I was dead, she says. I'm waiting for her to say, And I wish you were dead too I wish this whole fucking crowd the goddamn building would seize, but she doesn't.

The man sits on the floor. Folds his legs and crosses his ankles. We all stand without being asked. Even me.

The social worker paces the room, hyped-up; they've gone over this, I'm sure of it, it's part of a plan, a play. She can't trust him more than me, I tell myself. She can't trust he knows what to do. She's talking with her hands, rotating stretched palms and fists, and I'm wondering if she's worked up a sweat. Maybe this is therapeutic for her, I think. How nice. She keeps going round and round until she gets up behind me and says, I don't want to go.

I say, What did you say? But I heard her. Of course I did.

My foster dad, she says. He's being like, a total dick.

I'm sorry, I say. She waits pointedly and I ask what I can do to help.

I threatened to leave, she says. But I don't want to go.

Don't go, I say, and she waits and I try again. Do you want to stay?

I don't know, she says. But I don't want to go.

I understand, I say, and I do. Here I see relief in her eyes. We're close enough we can hold eye contact and I feel special, chosen, to have this intimacy with our leader. Too I feel disoriented; she remembers she didn't go over this with me, right? Then I tell myself it's because Rebecca and I have the home visit soon—an extra test to make sure we're ready.

I'll go with you, I say. Wherever you'd be happy. I'm thinking now would be a good time to impress her and use my wife's two-option coping skill but I can't get the framework straight in my head. Adrenaline is hitting and all I can think is don't go don't go don't go.

The social worker gives a nearly imperceptible nod;

that's probably not a good idea, promising to follow a person's anger until it meets its end. I feel betrayed, meaning I feel seen in the worst way. Run away with me, I am thinking. Come on. I imagine her blasting down the hallway and me clamoring after her. Babe, I'd say. Babe! We'd be all bent ankles and distorted hearing. People would be calling after us, quiet, though, not too bold or domineering, and we wouldn't look back. Our neighbors—I mean, our classmates—wouldn't quite know what to do. After all, who is prepared for a thing like that? A thing like what. A thing like a wound that isn't healing.

These hallways have a lot of double doors. They remind me of all my high schools, long and low public buildings without the automatic blocks in the event that someone has a gun. We should be more protected, I think, as I take the stairs down two at a time. Rebecca was a sprinter in college. Once after the intake session at a couples therapist, she told me she wished her mania set in on race days, something to give her that edge. It's dangerous to drink on your medication, I told her, because those were the days she was only *chilling out* when she was a few bottles deep. Otherwise, she was irritable, then angry, and I was a leach on her glimmers of a good mood. You're dangerous, she said, pitchy and, I guessed, correct.

We meet outside the building in the parking lot. I glance up and see our neighbors—classmates, classmates—observing from the window. The sun doesn't sit right in the sky for all of this to work: How can I see up at that angle, so clear, no squints, no neck arching, no saying, Jesus, it's bright? But I can. A few have phones to their ears and I can imagine what they're saying to dispatch: She went crazy, she bolted, no, no weapon but there's something off about her, it's all in the energy. It's all in the stance. At least one person holds their phone lower, steadied with both hands, and I'm wondering how many people are watching us live. I move to block Rebecca's face so we can keep this quiet—we don't need her program director to find out, don't need nasty students leaving reviews on that professor site. We don't need to be seen if we're not going to be understood.

Getting my hands on her face is not easy. She runs again and I chase again. We're knees up mouths open tongues dry faces damp. She's telling me to back the fuck up don't touch her don't fucking touch her and I'm crying, it's humiliating, but I'm having visions of her threats coming to real life—there are so many trucks trains bridges highways where a run and a jump would change it all. I want to call our neighbors down and tell them they're missing context. Everything is confusing when you're outside of the meat of the thing. What they need to know is Rebecca is decent at taking her antidepressants, okay? She's decent. I remind her, right. I do! We're not denying that. I wake her up before I go to work and I put the pill in her mouth. Otherwise, I ask her, and she says, I don't remember!! And then the brain zaps start up. Then she says she needs a drink to help. Then we might as well get the bigger bottle, it's a better deal, isn't it? I can't complain about money and force her to get so many little bottles when the big bottle is right there. I can't complain! She's right: I can't. The drinking and the antidepressants were bad, yeah. We know. But it's the psychiatrist's fault, too, on account of not realizing the pills are kickstarting the mania and the drinking and the yelling and look, the new pills are working. The new pills are fine. Why did I leave? Well. Well. I didn't know the new pills would work. I didn't know she'd get that prescription. No one mentioned it could be this other thing. No, I didn't google it. I don't know. Shit, I don't know. I wasn't thinking for myself, wasn't deducing a thing. I had all these parts and I couldn't touch my hand to any of it.

The neighbors ask the tough stuff: Would I have left if I had known? No. Would I have forgiven her if I had known? Of course. What about the experts who say a diagnosis not an excuse. Well, I'll let the experts be the experts. What about the people on the internet who would tell me I should have walked away the first time she did this or that or the other thing? The options the internet offered frightened me. I've never wanted to be without Rebecca, I've only wanted to be able to handle her.

Her hands hold my jaw for what I later realize must have been a while before I hear my name over and over. Name, nickname, name, nickname, first and last, nickname and last. I'm comforted, soothed. I realize the class is quiet, watchful. No one has a phone out but no one can look away. The social worker is talking to me and to them about words I've heard before: stress, emotional regulation, negotiation. I hear her talking about our hierarchy of needs and trauma responses. I realize I am sweating through my shirt and pants. I think there is sweat between my toes and definitely between my vulva and inner thighs. Clean me, I am thinking, but she keeps talking. We are back in the classroom and she is still talking about the same themes. I think she has done a great job of keeping everyone on task. I am wishing I could remember how she held our attention through the hallways and up the stairs. How she got everyone settled again.

It's like we never left.

Charlotte

26

CHARLOTTE HAS FOOD DELIVERED TO THE STU-
dio twelve hours after hearing from Olivia. She peed
three times before making the order, telling herself
that once she placed it, she'd hear from her friend who
would be angry she hadn't waited just a few more minutes. Charlotte orders Olivia's favorites: waffles with
oat whipped cream and dark chocolate chips on the
side, tamarind juice, a London fog with decaffeinated
tea. The food arrives and still nothing from Olivia—
her phone seems to be off. Dead, Charlotte's thinking.
Dead.

She's thinking luxury might revive Olivia, might send
her walking through the door, compelled by the feeling
of finally being missed and appreciated just the right
amount. She calls and asks about the plant-based high tea
from that place with topless women on the wall; no luck.

She looks up addiction treatment centers. She wonders if Rebecca would know what to do.

Her body feels weird and ugly, swollen. Her belly feels unnaturally heavy. Charlotte wonders if someone messed with it when she was asleep or having sex—did someone sew in bricks to weigh her down? At least the punishment would be time-consuming, worthy of what could be one's last living moments.

Charlotte uses marbles as the centers of her ghosts. She shapes the ghost-shaped sheets to drape over the marbles. The ghosts are artificial silk, smooth and disarming. The work is steady, good—the repetition feels exciting, not dull. How close to perfection can any one woman manage? Charlotte's ghosts are key chain trinkets. Olivia would be mortified if she knew, Charlotte thinks, twisting black wire into tiny legs, bends for the knees and feet. Little people hanging inside sheets. She carves out two holes and applies acrylic paint for the eyes—black runny pits that will dry poorly.

Charlotte imagines a girl defending her work in a seminar; the artist was meticulous her whole life (dramatic, Charlotte reasons with herself, but spirited) but we're not here because of what she did her whole life, we're here because of what she did when Olivia disappeared! Students will debate details; did Olivia disappear or was she taken? Was she hiding? Charlotte molds more ghosts, imagining horrors. She envies the young art history femmes of the future. They know what she doesn't—if her selfishness has already ended her life, if she's already lost the best of her loves.

She gets a text from Olivia saying she's waiting at a psych hospital down by the water. Charlotte sees missed calls, FaceTimes. She feels betrayed, confused; how can this happen so quickly? No texts.

Charlotte calls and it goes to voicemail. She calls the hospital and is put on hold. She calls back. She looks for a live chat option on the website. She looks up who owns the place, but only learns that it's a privately owned house of cards with two stars on Google.

They're about to take my phone, Olivia texts. *I'm waiting downstairs to be admitted.*

I'm so confused, Charlotte writes. *I thought you were finally home?*

My therapist is worried, Olivia says. *She kind of pushed me into it . . .*

Do you feel pressure? Remember you can leave . . .

Do you think I should leave before I sign anything?

Charlotte calls and it goes to voicemail.

A guy walks into the studio. He also has an iced coffee. He seems happy, well-adjusted. She wants to ask him about Olivia, millennial gay to elder gay. Charlotte runs through her actions in her head: she posted on Nextdoor, Facebook, and Craigslist. She directly messaged people with big verified accounts and tagged Olivia's profile with the words MISSING and NOT A DANGER TO OTHERS. Charlotte did not think about the possibility of Olivia getting into a car with a man, or on to the back of his motorcycle, or stumbling into an alley. Charlotte's vision includes a man throwing Olivia up into the air and her femur shattering on a raindrop. Olivia was supposed to be at home watching trivia and eating chickpea tofu. She isn't supposed to be worse.

Are you okay, he says. Can I help you find a chair?

Charlotte feels a temporary bliss. She loves fearful gay men. My angel, she thinks. She holds her stomach and allows herself to be led to a chair. He puts the paintbrushes on the floor and brushes the seat with his free hand.

I'm so scared about my friend, Charlotte says. She called me while I was here last night. She was outside of a bar . . . Charlotte is thinking *she was so hungry* but she can't say that to this stranger; he'll think she means Olivia was too poor to eat, and that's not correct. Charlotte is thinking hard about being correct because she hopes Olivia can feel her attention and that she will eat something and text her to come to her apartment. Charlotte sends her brain back to girlhood and attempts telepathy: you're my most important worry.

I'm so sorry, the stranger says. Where is she now?

The hospital, Charlotte says numbly. She's being admitted.

Wow, he says. Where?

Charlotte gives him a look and he puts his hands up. I Uber, he says. I do a lot of hospital pickups and drop-offs . . . Charlotte names the place and he nods, doesn't change his expression.

Does that seem like a good one, she asks. He looks around like he's comparing the local psychiatric facilities. After a silence he says, Do you . . . Were you going to take a car, or anything?

You're so sweet to offer, Charlotte says. But I don't

think I can see her right now. Charlotte doesn't know this. She found visitor hours listed on the website but she doesn't want to see Olivia alone.

You're sure? It's maybe twenty minutes, down by the twenty-four-hour McDonald's. His eagerness throws Charlotte for a second, but she dismisses it—all artists are lonely weirdos, especially in a community studio on a Sunday night.

The French place, Charlotte says, thinking of Olivia, how desirous she'd been to try the vegan croissant. She waits for him to say he really has to get some work done anyway but he doesn't, he just waits, and Charlotte feels like maybe going with him is a good idea. Olivia would walk if she had to, if the roles were reversed. Olivia wouldn't need a nudge.

If you really don't mind, Charlotte says. But I have to be a pain and use the restroom first, is that okay? He says, Sure, he's going to work until she's ready to head out. He heads to the glaze and Charlotte hides in the bathroom. She searches her texts for any contact information for anyone in Olivia's family, her parents or a cousin, but she finds nothing. She googles them with low expectations and finds nothing legitimate; her parents never got into computers, and if the others have social media, they seem to use names Charlotte doesn't know.

Standing in the otherwise-empty women's bathroom, three stalls with doors open and apricot soap and applicator-less tampons in a basket, Charlotte wants an adult. It occurs to her that either one of the Rebeccas might be helpful; her Rebecca has been put into those spaces, and Other Rebecca was the one who called it in once or twice, if Charlotte pieced the stories together accurately. The Rebeccas love to save. Charlotte refreshes Olivia's social media to see if she posted anything, or better yet, if someone else had commented on her pictures. Nothing; Charlotte isn't even sure Olivia has the apps on her phone anymore. She really doesn't care, Charlotte thinks. She's really alone.

Waiting outside the bathroom, Charlotte sees the scene in miniature; she's found bellyless and belly-up, and because fictional lumps of clay do more good than real cops, people ask some questions. Was she leading a double life? Was her life destroyed by an esoteric fetish? Would she have been better off in graduate school? The thought of postmortem exposure makes Charlotte want to die.

Any word, the guy says. Charlotte likes his patterned shirt, a floral button-down with cuffed short sleeves.

I've been thinking about my life, Charlotte begins. In episodes.

The man nods, smiles at Charlotte. She begins a slow walk to the door and he walks with her, jingling his keys. You're drinking coffee late, Charlotte says. She feels out of sorts. She wants someone to tell her to go home and rest—Olivia isn't going anywhere.

I try to stay up and drive before rush hour so I can sleep in peace, he says. Shake shake shake.

You know I really respect that, Charlotte says. I think that's a really good way to have control over your own life.

My own life, he says.

Frances Glessner Lee was like that, Charlotte says, though she has no idea if Lee was a night owl or ever drove a car. You know she came from a Harvard family? She wanted to go to medical school but of course women weren't allowed then. So she got married, had kids, and got a divorce. She made these dioramas, these crime scenes inspired by unsolved mysteries. Not all homicides, sometimes accidents or—

Let me pull around the car, he says.

Can I be honest, Charlotte says.

He says, Sure.

I'm nervous about seeing my friend, she says. I feel like she's maybe where she's supposed to be, I don't know? She's been hospitalized before, when we were teenagers, and to be honest I don't know the details but I have this feeling, like if I can sit down and map out our lives, can make it all really small and neat, we can fig—

Hey, he says. I'm so sorry to do this, but if we're going, we should get moving.

Maybe I want to stay, Charlotte says. I didn't ask you for a favor.

He laughs hard and loud. Babe, he says. You think I drive for *fun*? Mortified, Charlotte hands him two twenties for putting up with her, darts back into the women's bathroom, and requests an Uber home.

27

IN THE MORNING, I'M REMINDED OUR BUILDING doesn't have a working elevator and there's dog piss on the stairs. The social worker steps over it and nods when my wife and I speak over one another to reassure her this is a rarity. Rebecca explains the building's locks and the social worker appears to write this down, though I hadn't read anything specific to dead bolts. I'm thinking about Beatrice and her accidents; have they gotten more regular since I've moved out? Is that why we found vomit under the bed? Bea is a healthy, resilient dog, and I feel sick because something isn't right. And because I haven't eaten since the day before.

The social worker is the twin of my instructor; she is wearing a cap when we meet her outside, so I don't realize at first. She is smart, I decide. Sly. She doesn't introduce herself as a twin, obviously. She probably isn't even supposed to know who takes her sister's class. But I notice. Her name is different, though the moment she introduces herself it's gone from my mind. My wife and I welcome her inside and she accepts our suggestion of removing her shoes. Rebecca fusses over her tea choices (plain breakfast; soy milk if there's no whole in the fridge; a bit of sugar stirred in, bleached is fine) and I stand beside the couch and nod and smile.

I excuse myself into the bathroom and make the thirty steps from the kitchen, where the three of us are huddled, to the studio's one bathroom. I pass through our living room, our bedroom, our walk-in closet, and once inside the bathroom, I sit on the toilet.

Bea is in the tub with her toys. We've got a fan on her for some good air. She's asleep but unhappy, restless. It occurs to me we should get her checked sooner than later, but I don't know how to get her out without the social worker noticing. I think Heads or Tails; if Rebecca's been good with her pills, I'll ask Charlotte for help with the ride and bring the dog in myself. If Rebecca's been bad with her pills, I'll just take them all and lie down beside Bea.

I reach up and open the cabinet and try to see how many prescriptions Rebecca has filled without standing up. I don't want to crack my head open, I keep telling myself, but actually, I do.

I read and reread and reread. I use the calendar app on my phone to figure out how many pills she should have based on the pharmacy refill date on the bottles and after about ten minutes, I decide she's been taking the pills appropriately. I momentarily worry she's been flushing them under the pretense of taking them to appease me but I remind myself I am no longer living with her and she is no longer operating like a monitored beast. For good measure I root around behind the rolls of paper towels and toilet paper to see if she has any empty nips. She doesn't and so I emerge and put on a good face and hope we're getting a baby soon.

I must be unnerved by the social worker. Her hairline shines with sweat and I bet she washes with scented soaps: vanilla plum, cinnamon mango, burnt California. I hear myself lying about the air conditioner; it's off because it's broken, I tell her, but I add we're used to it, so sorry if she's uncomfortable, and she's saying, No, no, they're terrible for the environment anyway, and I'm nodding, I'm not telling her Rebecca uses it all the time with a bucket under it to catch the drip because it is broken and we're both too avoidant to email the landlord. One night after I left she was drunk and knocked over the bucket on her way to eat a granola bar. She said she woke up with chocolate smeared in her hands and panicked, thinking she'd shit herself. The curved plywood didn't seem as bad then.

We're big on climate change, Rebecca says. I mean, we're against it.

Right, the twin says, smiling.

We're not pro–climate change, I say, and neither of them laughs.

The first thing the twin asks us is if we live in a safe community and we say yes. I tell her we live walking distance to an elementary school, and I say a little extra to seem thoughtful and not foolish—of course the baby won't go to school, ha, ha, but there's a playground and a park and we can sit with the baby and teach the baby how to say *flower* and *mud* and *dirt*. Rebecca leans into me to signal she is pleased. The social worker asks us to talk about our extended families; are they supportive? Rebecca talks a long time about her mom and dad: ski trips as a family, a blueberry pancake recipe passed down from great-great-grandma, pronouns in their work emails. Neither of us mention her parents hate me. The twin turns to me and I tell her I'm actually not in touch with my family. I was in the system myself, on and off, over the years. Now that I'm stable, I tell her, I really want to give other kids what I didn't have growing up. Rebecca puts her hand on mine and my mind takes us to the set of a Lifetime movie where the whole room is thinking this moment is cliché, too neat, and the social worker brings us back to real.

How is your relationship, she says. Stability is important for these kids.

Great, we say.

How long have you been together, she says.

Five years, we say, and I chuckle when Rebecca adds the five months. She's right on, of course.

And your parents live a few states away, she says. Don't they? We nod. Rebecca included that information on our paperwork but I sense my wife's ruffled. The social worker asks us how our support network is here and who it involves.

Friends, Rebecca says. From my doctoral program and

my wife's job. Her classmates are frenemies at best, what with the department's competition over $3,000 summer grants and reimbursements for conference transportation each semester. All of them, including Rebecca, think they deserve to be at a better school with smarter people. I'm thinking about Rebecca's fake friends instead of my own because I don't think I have a friend outside of her. Charlotte crosses my mind and I smile at the wrong moment.

I hate to ask the same question again, the twin says. But it's important. We nod and she says it's not good communication and she knows she shouldn't do it; I'm saying it again to get a different answer, she explains and we nod, and she asks us again about our relationship.

All good in your marriage, she says. We nod and she asks how we handle conflict.

We look at one another, relieved; this is the sort of question we're prepared to answer. I tell myself I'm paranoid thinking she's found my profile on the app or talked to Charlotte on the sidewalk. My wife is really patient, Rebecca explains. She's cool and calm in an emergency.

I learned such great communication from her, I say. I lower my voice and say it was difficult, at first, living in a safe home but I've learned how to regulate my big feelings and I don't want to run away anymore. I add that we don't go to bed angry and am reminded of the time Rebecca hid my keys and medicine and locked me out of our apartment building. She found me hours later, pissing in a bush right outside. I hadn't tried to find anywhere else to go, hadn't made her work at all to find me, and when she led me into the elevator, we both said we were sorry. I don't tell the twin and instead tell her again we're so grateful we're being considered on the fast track.

Every day a baby doesn't have a home is a tragedy, I say. When she smiles, I make a mental note to leave an encouraging comment on the YouTube video I stole that sentence from.

And it's just the two of you, she says. Who will parent the baby?

Right, Rebecca says, and I can feel she's unsettled at the implication of these questions.

This is both of our first marriage, I tell the twin. No ex-husbands or boyfriends hanging around.

We're both gay, Rebecca says. Really gay.

The social worker nods and writes something down. We all laugh with our mouths, no eyes or cheeks.

The rest of the morning goes that way: on and on and on. What is our discipline philosophy (feelings first!) what do we think about charter schools (protect public education!) what are our thoughts on children doing chores (the only chore the baby will have is to smile, ha, ha!) when was the last time we traveled outside the country (never as a couple) how secure are your jobs (the wife practically has tenure, so . . .) do you have any health issues (let's just say one of us has to limit her sweet tooth) what are your hopes for this child or any you foster (a life better than ours). She asks about our upbringings and Rebecca describes softball camp and Spanish-immersion summer school and trips to New York all the way from her home state of West Virginia. I knew I'd end up there, she tells the twin, and the truth is, she did, and so I did, too. The social worker doesn't ask why we don't live in New York, saving us the explanation of postdocs, and asks me to describe the best and worst moments of my childhood.

Oh, I tell her. I was in the system. This time, her face doesn't change.

I understand it can be heavy to talk about, she says. But I have to ask.

Right, I say. Well, yeah. It was a long time ago and it's over now. To her silence I add that I did some therapy as an adolescent to help with those scary emotions I couldn't name (I never went, but she can't get those kind of records) and that my life is so different now, I never think about it.

What was the worst moment of your childhood, she says. The doorbell rings and no one moves to get it.

Um, I tell her. You know, I really don't remember.

Accessing those memories can be hard, Rebecca says. It's like, traumatic.

Right, I mimic. Traumatic.

Try, she says. It's a safe space. Your home, she says. It's a safe space. Her pen is ready to write and I give her a good story. An uncle at home—yes, a real uncle, yes, blood uncle, this was one of those temporary situations where I stayed with my mother's estranged sister while my parents were in jail—molested me. I don't go for *inappropriate touches* or *funny business*. The social worker doesn't flinch and I don't look to see Rebecca's reaction. I had my own bedroom and kept the door open no matter what I was doing because I was afraid everyone would sneak out the front door and set the house on fire and I didn't want to die before I started high school. The uncle got real quiet in the hallways by my bedroom and especially the bathroom when I was in the tub with the door open knees to my chest to hide my puffed breasts. I flitted around in two towels because I was young but not stupid. He molested me anyway by insisting on giving me back rubs when his wife was downstairs making some boxed mac and cheese for everybody.

He did it a couple of times, the same way, him standing behind me and me frozen in front of my desk, staring down at the math homework I didn't know how to do (maybe this is why I never figured out pre-algebra, ha, ha). His hands were flat palms against my breasts once they got down there from my shoulders.

I read an advice column in *Teen Vogue* about what to do if you're molested and I figured it would give me a lot of options but there was really just one: Tell your parents right now. I told my aunt and she told him to be more careful and he came up to my room and apologized and gave me another back rub and moved all the way down my front to the top of my underwear, where he got himself a few curls of pubic hair. I moved all around in a circle and he stuck on to me like we were playing a puppet game. I bluffed and told him I'd seen the videos he downloaded on the computer and he didn't touch me again but he looked at me long and hard until I got moved to a non-blood family on account of my aunt getting caught with drugs in her car during a traffic light stop.

Those were hard years, I say.

And the best moments, the twin prompts, unruffled and writing all the while.

I give her one of my rare star-smiles and mimic her ease; the trauma is so far gone, I don't cry or tense or ask for a moment to collect myself. Talking about meeting my wife doesn't build my throat up into the top of my mouth, doesn't take root in my molars. I imagine my bile crusting on the insides of my ears, saying hello to the wax. I describe the bus to New York I was on in the hours before my future wife approached me on a sidewalk in Queens. I was moving to the city to get out of a different relationship. The bus broke down by several hospitals. I kept asking people if I could take the train to get to Staten Island and everyone just smiled. I didn't understand the city enough to understand why I was amusing. I texted Rebecca because I didn't have the number of anyone else who lived in New York. She explained how to get on the bus and transfer to the other bus and then the train. She reassured me it would be the last stop. She asked if I knew about the ferry and I reassured her I did but she typed deleted typed deleted typed deleted then told me to wait there and she would meet me. I waited with my backpack and suitcase and duffle bag. I was too gauche to go into the store and buy a bottle of water so when she arrived forty minutes later I really did feel speechless. She didn't have a drink with her—it wasn't that movie perfect, ha, ha—but she walked me several blocks in a direction I wouldn't have gone and bought me a MetroCard. It's confusing, she said, both of us staring at the machine. She used her debit card instead of letting me spend $2.75, as though she already knew. On the subway she talked about herself and we joked about how weird it was, this coincidence, of the two of us actually being so close on my first day in this big city. On the app we'd both said we were looking for dyke sex, casual, no big feelings, and by the time I was on the ferry and she was headed to her studio in Astoria, I figured I'd be moving in by fall. We married before the feds even recognized us.

Charlotte

28

CHARLOTTE DOESN'T SEE OLIVIA'S PARENTS IN
the lobby. She looks for someone who resembles her small
friend—a cousin, an aunt, a grandparent—and reads the
names on the visitor log while the receptionist checks her
ID. No one sounds familiar.

Wait, the receptionist says after passing Charlotte a
sticker. It doesn't say *visitor*. It doesn't say anything.

I'm sorry, Charlotte says. She senses her blank face
won't work here.

Wait, the receptionist repeats, louder. She gestures to
rows of chairs.

Charlotte hesitates. She doesn't want to wait, she wants
to see Olivia. She wants to check her texts. It's my first time
here, Charlotte says. I'm not sure what I'm waiting for.

You're waiting because I told you to, the receptionist
says. I'll tell you when it's your turn.

Charlotte startles. She makes a note to write a complaint about this person later, though their name tag isn't filled out. Remember her face, Charlotte thinks. And the time of day.

May I have my phone back, Charlotte says, feeling silly. While I wait?

The receptionist sighs. She looks over her shoulder at the case where she has placed Charlotte's phone among the others. Charlotte maintains eye contact with the woman while she calls for the next person in line and Charlotte air-slices her into bits.

Olivia is wearing a big sweatshirt and sweatpants. The entire outfit is gray. She's in big white socks and no shoes. The girls embrace without speaking. Charlotte smells soap on Olivia and in her hair.

Who do I call to get you out, Charlotte says. There's a large television hanging in one corner of the room. Five or six adults are sitting on the floor, watching couples on a game show. Charlotte can't imagine how people go onto these things; she doesn't know half the answers about herself, and even if she did, she can't imagine trusting herself not to change her answer.

I don't know, Olivia says. I'm waiting to be evaluated by a psychiatrist.

Did a regular doctor see you first, Charlotte says and Olivia shakes her head no.

No one's seen me yet, she says. They gave me something to knock me out after I had an explosion in line for the phone.

That doesn't sound like you, Charlotte says. I'm so sorry.

You are my emergency contact, Olivia continues. On my insurance.

Charlotte nods. You haven't called your parents, she says. Or they're on their way?

I'm not calling them, Olivia says seriously. I'm not ever going to call them.

Charlotte nods again. Once the doctor sees you, can you leave? They're probably going to give you something to keep you . . . mild. Charlotte is dying to know what Olivia said to end up here. Did an overeager clinician push her off to a facility just because she's sad? Because she got too drunk at a gay bar? Who hasn't! Charlotte wants to know and she cannot ask because she does not believe she can live with the consequences of knowing.

The doctor will put me on a new medication, Olivia says. They'll monitor it . . .

When do I come and get you, Charlotte says. Do you need me to call anyone and tell them you'll be out?

I don't know, she says. They didn't tell me anything.

You're cold, Charlotte says. The hairs on your arms are up . . .

We can't adjust the temperature in our rooms, she says. We can't adjust the blinds. We can't open the windows. No laces. No nail clippers. No scarves . . .

I'll bring you sweatshirts tonight, Charlotte says. Are they checking bags? They hustled me a little on my way in . . . At Olivia's blank stare, Charlotte says she'll follow the rules. No strings, no zippers.

I'm so worried for you, Charlotte says. I don't think this place is helping.

Olivia says nothing.

I just don't understand how it got this bad, Charlotte continues. I thought you were actually doing better ... Olivia stays silent and Charlotte says she wants to help. Tell me what to do, she says. Tell me what to do to keep you safe outside this hellhole.

Olivia snaps her head up at this offer, appearing relieved. Get into my email, she says. Update everyone, all my pending projects. Can you see if my income qualifies me for anything? Maybe get on the phone with my insurance ...

Charlotte does not want to do any of these tasks. I'm really worried about you, she says. Is there something I don't know?

How would I know what you know, Olivia says. I don't know what I know.

I'm scared, she says. I don't think I really know what to do.

Charlotte, Olivia says.

Yeah, Charlotte says.

Get the fuck out.

What, Charlotte says. There's only like, an hour left—

The girls roll around on the floor for a minute or two before they're broken up. A couple other residents get involved, pulling at arms and legs, but mostly people are excited. It's a little action, a little heat. Both women are crying because they're mad and don't know how else to express it. The security guards don't let them make up or talk it out. Charlotte's never been removed from a place before, never been walked to the door. Olivia's red crying face turns around in Charlotte's head while she waits for one of the two guards to get her phone; she's warned that she could be arrested, that what took place was an assault, that she's being let off easy, don't come back. Charlotte gets tears out and nods her understanding.

We have your picture, the receptionist reminds her in the lobby. We know.

CHARLOTTE USES HER spare key to get into Olivia's and packs sweatshirts, socks, sports bras, underwear, a rechargeable bullet vibrator, toothpaste. Are they allowed floss? Charlotte has to breathe well. Olivia doesn't belong there, she thinks. How did she get so bad?

Can you hurry, her Rebecca has texted. *I will do anything*

Please

Please

Please

Charlotte vowed not to respond until she dropped off Olivia's stuff at the next session of visiting hours. She's not exactly sure how she's going to get it up there, with it being the same people at the door, but she figures at least they'll bring the bag up. They can't make Olivia suffer; isn't the whole point of the place to make her happy?

Charlotte puts her belly on and her papier-mâché project in the back seat of Olivia's car. She doesn't input a destination.

29

I FIDDLE WITH DETAILS, OF COURSE. I DON'T MEN-
tion the woman back in my college town who I let email
the bus company a complaint after it deserted us miles
from our destination. I don't mention the sex app. Rebecca and I met through friends, I say, and she nods, our
old story for the straights, it's like we're at a faculty party
and she's the new fellow and I'm her wife. We've always
been good at making ourselves palatable to the heteros
even if we'd spent the Lyft to the event bickering about
changing passwords and exhausting heavy sighs. And Rebecca isn't going to add texture to my story; we're both
thinking of the eating disorder she used to self-destruct
before adding alcohol, all the walking she was doing
when she got out of work as an assistant at a law office
at the precise moment I, then just a flirty icon, asked for
her help. Neither of us asked each other why the other

was there when we reached out in our small loneliness. We both knew.

The longer I talk about Rebecca, the easier it is to forget she is going to leave me. Rebecca, I think, wants me home but not enough to ask me. This makes me feel guilty until I think about Rebecca overdrafting our joint checking account to buy jumbo slices or the time she woke up in bed at the inpatient unit of a mental health hospital and told me she regretted ever knowing me. I brought her a bottle of orange juice from a vending machine and when I offered to open the juice, Rebecca put her hands around my neck and squeezed. Not an hour later, she confessed to the nurse.

The nurse asked me to leave more than once before she told me she'd have to get security. Let's give this some space, she said. Everyone's got to go to bed. We were in the hallway and I was imagining Rebecca spider crawling toward the automatic doors.

It's just playing, I said, and the nurse interrupted me when I said Rebecca was still drunk and hadn't refilled her medication and her childhood dog was getting old and her term papers were due and she had to get references for her thesis and I was always leaving the windows open with the air on and there's no nightmare like a D.C. summer and she thinks she gained a lot of weight she thinks I gained a lot of weight she thinks beer is a fine breakfast for adults but not dramatic babies like me.

Rebecca called me a few hours after. I sat in our apartment and listened to our neighbor vacuum. She was crying and thought I'd disappeared and abandoned her;

we went back and forth, speaking over one another to re-assure ourselves we didn't leave, we thought we had been left.

I tell the twin that Rebecca's the best mother I know, and they both laugh, and I feel good.

She changed my whole life, I say, and Rebecca says, You too, and the social worker nods but doesn't write it down. I text Charlotte again, asking if she can get Olivia to help get Bea to a vet, any vet.

When it comes to baby arrival, the social worker's all business. There's not a square footage minimum, no; the baby can sleep in our bedroom in the pack and play or the crib or whatever we're using. Rebecca asks about co-sleeping and the lady repeats the baby needs at least the pack. We read all this online already, separately, both of us in bed with screens just beyond our noses. The twin tells us not to paint the walls pink or blue though we can if we really want to; gender-neutral is better, she says, like a white or tan or beige. We don't point out we aren't allowed to paint a rental apartment and I, at least, ap-preciate she pretends to take us seriously—we could be homeowners in some version of this life. A night light is a must for fosters of all ages, she continues. Even the teen-agers. Art is good and the baby can pick it out with you. Rebecca chuckles at this and for the first time during the meeting the twin scowls.

These kids can't choose you, she says. Giving them ev-ery other choice helps them love you.

I want to be loved and so I tell her I agree, The baby totally needs to pick their own wall art. I tell a story about all the galleries in Dupont, how we'll take the baby in one of those sacks strapped to Rebecca's chest and we'll let the baby signal to us which paintings they like the best. If they fall asleep in a store we can't afford, I'll steal some prints, but I keep that plan to myself.

Rebecca asks about toiletries but it's not a question; she mentions having read in the *Foundations of Fostering* brochure that we'll need pacifiers, diapers, formula, bottles, binkies, wipes, and ointments on hand; does the agency have any insight into the best or safest brands? She's messing with the twin now, showing off that she's smart and prepared. I know she thinks the baby art is bullshit and I hope she decides it's the social worker who is an uptight bitch and not me.

I get worried about Rebecca getting mad when the twin leaves. I go into my head a little then a little more then a little more and then I'm gone. The twin and Rebecca are speaking and I'm not moving. Rebecca and I are on the futon we call a couch and the social worker is at the folding desk chair we got while a neighbor was moving out. Rebecca was happy when I pointed out the furniture before it hit the curb; less chance of inheriting someone's bugs. The chair is black and a little dinged but I don't think the twin has noticed. When she talks about the chair directly I think I am spinning out; she suggests blankets and a pillow and I get up as though to grab some from a closet but in reality the only bedding we have is attached to our mattress.

Ha ha ha, the two of them laugh at me and Rebecca

tugs me back down beside her. Her hand is warm and not angry. I sit.

For when the baby is here, the twin says. You'll want to make the chair comfortable for you.

I ask why, too disoriented to be shy.

The baby will feel better when you feel better, she says. They'll know if you're tense.

Great, I say. Great!

The social worker ignores my enthusiasm and speaks quickly. There are many items we need to buy—donated is fine, we shouldn't think we're too good for Goodwill, because we're not, she stresses, and I nod, full obedience—and we need to make sure there's room for everything in this apartment. Total rookie mistake to assume babies don't need room, she tells us. Rebecca moves to her standing desk and begins to demonstrate how she intends to take it down to make room for a pack and play when the knocking at the door returns. We all freeze: There is emotion in those knocks. But we have been waiting for just this sort of crisis to remind us of how good we feel when we're against a world.

30

I LOVE YOU, CHARLOTTE TELLS HER STOMACH. You're not alone. She repeats this refrain up the stairs, around the dog piss, down the hall, and at the door. You're not alone. You're not abandoned. Olivia's spare car key is in her pocket; she reasons that if Olivia came home and wanted to drive, it wouldn't be safe in her condition. She left a note on Olivia's whiteboard: a big question mark and a sketch of her car with a dog behind the wheel. Charlotte imagines Olivia stumbling home and eating an entire box of organic animal crackers. She'd laugh at this picture. Nap right on the tile.

Charlotte stands outside her Rebecca's door and listens; they're scrambling inside, Bea is whining, and the Rebeccas might be arguing—she can't entirely discern the whispers, but she feels the urgency. The social worker hasn't left yet and Charlotte has no explanation for her interruption. Other Rebecca's direction was clear: *wait outside in the car.* You can take yourself away, she thinks. She knocks on the door.

She's still here, her Rebecca says in the hallway outside her apartment door. I'm so sorry, she whispers, but the social worker is still inside.

I'm having a loss, Charlotte says. I'm alone.

Call someone, her Rebecca hisses. Your friends.

Olivia's in the hospital, Charlotte says. She realizes she is crying very hard.

Look, her Rebecca says. Can you wait at a Starbucks or something? She lowers her voice: My ex is here, okay? The social worker is here. Do you understand? You need to be somewhere else right now.

I'm dying, Charlotte says. What she means is: Everything is changing.

You're not dying, her Rebecca says, kindergarten-teacher like. You're doing a great job, okay? I asked you to come help Bea, okay? Can you wait outside? Please?

Charlotte says, Sure, and then scoots around her Rebecca and enters the apartment.

Hi, Other Rebecca says. She's speaking to Charlotte like everything is normal; why can't your wife be like this, Charlotte thinks. Why can't she play pretend? She gives the social worker a really sad look.

This is our friend, the other Rebecca continues. Her name is Charlotte, and she's actually having a baby soon herself. Another voice drifts into the design set of Charlotte's mind; someone saying I can see that and then all three women laughing. Charlotte personally thinks the third woman, the social worker, could look a little more engaged in the whole thing. Charlotte tightens her grip on her belly—no one is stealing her baby. She's no stupid bitch, she thinks.

I'm so sorry to do this, Charlotte says, though she isn't sorry at all. But I have to interrupt your appointment.

Is everything okay, the social worker asks. She sounds concerned, which encourages Charlotte.

No, Charlotte says. I'm having . . . pains.

Pains, the women repeat. Pains?

I need to go to the hospital, Charlotte says quietly. I need to go right away.

Are you bleeding, the other Rebecca asks. What happened?

A man threatened me, Charlotte says. With a gun. The social worker gasps. Charlotte has to think, Don't smile don't smile don't smile. She manages each word as if she has the power of a god. I threw my wallet, she says, though her wallet is actually in her tote bag. And he ran off, you know, but I'll never forget his look . . .

It's okay, the social worker says. That sounds very scary. Did he touch you?

Only with his eyes, Charlotte says, feeling a little glum; she wants the Rebeccas to whisk her away. She doesn't want to be analyzed by someone who doesn't understand their game. Questions about her safety take away from the point—she's a damsel in distress, sure. But she made it home. She made it to her women. Doesn't that count for something?

I'm heading to my next appointment, the social

worker says to the other Rebecca. But can I take you to our office? I can drop you off.

Office, Charlotte says, pitchy.

There are advocates, the social worker says. They can help you process and consider your options.

Options, Charlotte says. She can't remember if it's a crime to file a fake police report. She looks at the social worker and is disappointed; the woman seems kind and normal, the sort of person who would drive someone in need to a place they had to go. She wishes she could ask her to find Olivia but she doesn't want to give up the attention or accept Olivia is gone at all. Behind the social worker, both Rebeccas are looking at her with terrified expressions.

It's up to you, the social worker says. You're the survivor.

Let me walk you to your car, her Rebecca says. My wife will stay with—

Your friend needs you, the social worker says. I understand. Implicit in her voice: What I don't understand is why you aren't taking her pain more seriously. Charlotte appreciates this approach; after all, how are the Rebeccas going to parent if they can't even prioritize a friend who was just held at gunpoint? A pregnant friend, at that. She could be spotting from the stress! She takes in a slow, low gasp for effect.

Thank you for being so understanding, Other Rebecca says. Your patience is a lifesaver. Charlotte allows a little smile to creep into her face; of course Other Rebecca is better at pretending, better at acting along with social graces. Her Rebecca isn't used to having to bend this way, to pretend she's fine with not getting what she wants. The shift in her loyalties confuses her, but maybe, she thinks, that's her denial at work. Which woman does she know? Certainly not herself.

Olivia, she says out loud. That's the woman she knows. And where is she? Alone.

Olivia, the social worker repeats. Is that your name? Or the baby's?

The baby's, the women lie in unison. It's the baby's name. And Charlotte shines. Her eyes are wet, her mouth feels small and dry, and her shoulders shake. They quiver. She's feeling good in the hallway because the social worker is almost unbearably attentive. Should she sit? Does she want a water with ice? What about tea? The other Rebecca has started fussing around Bea, who is whimpering. The social worker and her Rebecca nod, and smile, and shake hands, and then Charlotte is alone with her Rebeccas.

Hurry up, she repeats. Bea is so goddamn sick.

It's got to be that plant, the other Rebecca is saying. It's all in her vomit. Her Rebecca responds to this by saying fuck fuck fuck with a red face. Charlotte wonders if she'll be mad enough to hit.

I'm really sorry, Charlotte says carefully. I told her to check.

Who is her, the other Rebecca asks. God?

Olivia, Charlotte says.

Your mentally ill friend, her Rebecca fills in. That's who you put in charge of reading the instructions?

She's really smart, Charlotte says. She's not sick like that. We can go to Old Town, she suggests. It's where my parents bring their dogs.

We might need another location, the other Rebecca blurts. Like, a nonprofit.

You don't, Charlotte says. I've got it. The other Rebecca shakes her head in protest but her Rebecca says a hurried thank-you without eye contact.

Do we need to carry Bea, her Rebecca says in lieu of greater celebration of Charlotte's generosity. Can she stand?

Charlotte prods into her hind legs and the dog exhales. Her big brown eyes look cloudy and fatigued. Please don't die, Charlotte says.

The three women carry Bea outside with little dignity. She leaks diarrhea and the women lament their circumstances along with her. Charlotte has her hind legs. Her tail is curled up against her stomach like she's trying to keep puppies inside. Charlotte doesn't know how to tell if she's fixed.

31

I'M SHITTING MY PANTS THE WHOLE TIME WE'RE on the road. Charlotte swears up and down it's fine with Olivia that we take her car, but when my wife asks to see Charlotte's driver's license *just in case* Charlotte says she doesn't have her wallet on her but it's fine. I hold my seat belt with my left hand and my wife's hand with my right. We don't care about Charlotte's license; we're worried about the vet bill. Bea is curled up between us in the middle seat, quiet and afraid. I pray that this office is fancy enough to accept Apple Pay.

Someone needs to say something, my wife says. I can't handle this quiet. Charlotte turns up the volume of a podcast and I groan. Never mind, my wife says. Jesus Christ.

Hi, Bea, Charlotte calls from the front seat.

How does everyone know each other, my wife says, and I want us to swerve into brick.

Olivia, I say. The girl who owns this car? The one in the hospital? I know her because she's friends with Charlotte. And I know Charlotte because we've been spending time together the last couple of weeks. As I speak, I wonder how it's only been that long. Everything feels accelerated.

Hmm, my wife says. She pats Bea's head. And how did you meet, she says. Her voice sounds strained and controlled, like she is giving boarding announcements for a rocket designated to explode for the pleasure of the rich and perverse. I flex the door handle and Charlotte presses a button up front.

Hands on our laps, she says. Please.

Charlotte, my wife says. Tell me.

Um, Charlotte says. She says she has to concentrate on getting over the bridge. We are in traffic, not moving much. I ask where Olivia is, hoping it seems like we're all just great friends, and Charlotte says she is actually in the hospital.

Olivia is hospitalized right now, my wife repeats dryly. Really?

Bea is sick, Charlotte repeats. But so is Olivia.

Their intimacy confuses me; they're speaking as though they know one another, but I can't piece it together. Charlotte followed me, sure. But Charlotte's never mentioned working the program, and her weird little friend never mentioned knowing another Rebecca, either. What's the connection? It's easier to try and figure this out than to figure out what I am going to offer as an explanation for my hideous behaviors.

And how did you know Olivia was in the hospital, my wife says.

I try not to move any of the muscles in my face. I hope we die and Bea doesn't.

Can you drop us off at the vet and *then* see Olivia, my wife presses. Charlotte leaving makes me nervous, because I don't know how we'll pay without her, and because I don't want my wife to freak once we're alone.

Charlotte turns the podcast back up.

Tell me, my wife says. Tell me anything.

I can't look at her face. I can't look at Bea, who is whining louder and louder. Traffic lulls to a stop on the bridge and we're in the middle. We've all been in the district long enough to have had this happen before; it's only the Potomac, only underpaid interns hustling back to the suburbs. But I really want to die.

Maybe someone else should drive, I say. Too much stress for the baby. My wife scoffs beside me.

I think my blood pressure is dropping, Charlotte says, and her need jolts my wife and me into action; Rebecca lowers her window to let some air in and Charlotte doesn't complain about the lost air-conditioning. I hold on to the dog, still afraid she's going to die right then and there, but I'm grateful, too, so grateful. I never know what to say for myself because I would never accept any answer I can offer.

I've been doing what I need to do to build a family, my wife says in the silence. Do you understand what I'm saying?

I don't, but I tell her I do. There are many things I don't want to know, like why she said *a* family instead of *our* family. I ask how she knows Charlotte.

Can we just have quiet, Charlotte says. Can we just drive?

I whisper to my wife, asking where the plant that got Bea sick came from and my wife says it was a surprise, a gift.

She said it was safe for dogs, my wife whispers back. She promised.

Bea needs help, Charlotte says resolutely once we're inside the vet's lobby. My wife looks ashamed. I don't recognize my reflection in the windows. I never do.

I hear my wife ask Charlotte if she can talk to her *over there*, and I pretend not to watch them cross the room to a cluster of chairs. Someone in magenta scrubs is talking to me and I'm not listening. The tech is already holding Bea's leash and rubbing her ears. I have no purpose here.

I have great news, my wife says. They'll accept Apple Pay. She's beside me and the tech is smiling and nodding at her; my wife's so good at being normal. I can imagine my wife smoothing over any reason to be in an emergency room; she could convince a nurse a baby's tumble came from a little too much momentum on the slide instead of a little too hard of a push. I feel hands on my back and I think: Hi, Mom.

I don't mind, Charlotte says in the background of my fantasy world. I planned to pay. For what, I'm thinking, and too, I'm nodding, relieved, and I'm thinking, How the hell am I getting so lucky? I'm wondering if this is all they discussed in the corner; doesn't Rebecca want to know how Charlotte knows her wife? Doesn't she sense the truth? I think of rats finding their way home by following their own trail of grease, the inevitable reversal of a hero's journey. What are the odds, I'm thinking. How can anyone be so oblivious?

I'll give you a call when we settle the bill, the tech says. It shouldn't go above this amount. The estimate is in the five figures. It's more than we have in our bank accounts combined. Charlotte says that's fine. She hardly blinks.

You're a wonderful friend, the receptionist says.

It's the least I can do, Charlotte says. Since I've been sleeping with her wife.

The receptionist chuckles. She has big eyes that get bigger but if she senses any truth to Charlotte's confession, she doesn't show it. The receptionist staples a receipt to a treatment plan and passes the papers to Charlotte.

Can we talk outside, my wife says. I'm thinking: Me? Charlotte nods and we follow her.

Charlotte and I have had an arrangement, my wife begins. I didn't want to tell you because I didn't think it was good for you to know. She is looking at me seriously with wide eyes. I realize I am someone she is trying to please and I feel, temporarily, powerful.

She isn't really pregnant, my wife adds. Obviously.

Are you joking, I say. Are you messing with me? I'm thinking: I thought we wouldn't talk about this. I thought we might have loved each other. It's that weird, that destabilizing.

I don't know what I was thinking, she says. I just want a family.

A family, I repeat. Part of me knows I'm focusing on the wrong thing but I stomp that sliver out. I say, We are a family, and she stares at me and I would give more than a whole lot to be inside her head.

I'm your family, I tell her. We are a family.

You left, she says. I did everything because you left.

I didn't think you'd get sober around me, I say. I felt like I was driving you to drink, you were so unhappy.

I was unhappy with my whole life, she says. Drinking nightly on mood stabilizers didn't help.

Nightly, I say. It did get to that, didn't it? Buying wine in jugs as a better deal, saving a beer for the mid-morning scramble before getting out the door.

Leaving Bea's been impossible, I say. The words feel bad and ugly in my mouth. I really hate myself.

I'm really sorry to do this, Charlotte says. But I need one of you to help me with Olivia.

My wife does not turn. Charlotte repeats herself. I can't go inside the building, she starts. We got into a scuffle but Olivia needs a bunch of stuff . . .

Are we interchangeable, my wife says. As long as someone is giving you attention, it doesn't matter who?

That's not what I mean, Charlotte says. I'm just trying—

You're good, my wife says. We'll take a car home with Bea later.

It's so expensive, Charlotte says. All the way out here.

Charlotte, my wife says. Go.

I keep looking down; I wonder if the receptionist can

hear us from inside. I hope the doors are too heavy for sound to travel that well. I feel small and sick and a little relieved—I won't have to imagine being trapped. I never let myself get that far. And I only have to live it once.

I don't know what to say, I tell both of them. I feel like I'm watching us on TV.

No, my wife counters. You don't get to leave me with no information. I open my mouth to tell her I didn't ask her anything, but she fills in the space and says I don't get to decide that for everyone.

I was hooking up with Charlotte because I wanted to feel powerful, I say. My voice is small and the words come slowly; I'm not good enough, not pure-intentioned enough to get the words out fast and ease the pain. I think I will have to repeat myself but my wife just says, Okay, right. She says I was right; she would have preferred not knowing.

And you've been saving the money she gave you, my wife says slowly. For the baby?

Charlotte actually hasn't given me money, I admit.

I'm confused, my wife says. I think the rage under her skin is going to send her to the moon. I want to hold her around the middle and find stars with her. There's a long silence, and because I'm a bad person, I let Charlotte speak for me. She explains I was pretending to be a sugar mommy but obviously that didn't work and here we are.

You tried to kill Bea by bringing that plant, my wife says. You interrupted our meeting. Your friend is in the hospital. Now you need us to leave our dog so we can help you, what? Seem like a better person than you actually are?

I didn't try to kill anyone, Charlotte says. You said we're getting rid of the dog. She turns to me and informs me her money wasn't going only to the baby stuff but to renting a new place so my wife wouldn't live with memories of me.

You're being cruel, my wife says. What is the point of this?

You're being fucking weird, I add. Fuck.

I'm not weird, Charlotte says. You're weird for hanging on to a dog you got when you were together. You're so transparent.

My wife and I say, Transparent? I add that of course we're going to take care of our dog. It's our dog.

You're irresponsible, Charlotte says. You want a baby but you can't take care of a dog? You didn't have the means for the dog to begin with. You're playing at being a family but you can't take care of yourselves.

I know, my wife says. But so are you.

What do you mean, I say.

Nothing, my wife says. Don't listen to her.

Her, Charlotte repeats loudly. Her?

Come on, I say. I like Charlotte. I'm not trying hard, I'm coasting, I'm wondering if I'll really get out of this without being the monster—you don't end up in the system unless you're the smallest monster, unwanted by every aunt and uncle and cousin. A good person wouldn't have the bruises in my blood.

Why do you like Charlotte, my wife asks. She looks to be trying very hard to stay calm.

She's funny, I say. Well-intentioned . . . creative, imaginative . . .

Babe, my wife says. She's a fucking basket case.

Every basket case needs a family, I say, because I am thinking what if I am actually the basket case and everyone abandons me because I am inherently unlovable, a mistake on this shriveling planet? And I've been a little happier lately, a little enlivened—maybe it's the limerence, maybe it's the time spent in the sun. I'm telling myself everything is fine, everything is fine.

I felt really safe, Charlotte says. You filled in the details of each other for me. I didn't have to guess what you really wanted, or try to figure out who you really were. It was comforting not to second-guess.

When I hit Charlotte across the face, she doesn't put her hands up. I beat on her stomach, grab her hard and roll us around. I couldn't feel dumber, couldn't be dumber. My wife says she can't stand to watch us act like this, she's going inside, she's going to ask about our Bea baby. On the ground, we cry like kids.

Charlotte

32

THE WORLD DIDN'T REACT MUCH WHEN CHAR-
lotte was hit dead in the face; she stumbled back and
let herself fall to make sure the ground was still there.
No strangers poked their heads out. No cars slowed. She
thinks: People probably thought we were sisters.

Charlotte stands up. Her head and arms and legs are
back together, the thick clump of her torso holding her as
upright as any other day.

It's funny, Other Rebecca—Only Rebecca, she tries in
her head, Only Rebecca—says. She stays on the ground,
talks with gravel still in her hands.

What's funny, Charlotte says. Her body already hurts.
She wants to check her belly but she doesn't want to reig-
nite Rebecca's violence.

I wouldn't have minded if you'd just told me, she says.
If you'd been like, Oh, as a heads-up, this is not a real baby.

I guess you're a more accepting person than I am, Charlotte says. Your wife didn't take it as well.

And that's where I came in, Rebecca says. Did I measure up?

To what?

To what my wife said about me… You must have come in with some kind of knowledge.

I don't know, Charlotte says. I'm always living a better, more interesting life in my head.

Liar, Rebecca says. Scaredy cat.

Charlotte gets onto all fours on the street and charges Rebecca. The ground is warm and damp, like it'd been freshly christened with rain or urine. Your wife, Charlotte thinks, she said you're an angel, you can forgive anything… Maybe I was wondering, can she forgive this? The pavement is hot, she stage-whispers in real life.

Imagine webs are coming out of my fingers, Rebecca says and Charlotte, still on the ground, nods. Woosh, Rebecca says, making her voice like a ghost. Oooooh. Charlotte tramples around, rubbing her palms and knees raw, and Rebecca waves her arms, directing as though Charlotte is an orchestra, not just one odd woman. It feels good getting their bodies up and down and around. Rebecca doesn't excuse herself when she jogs across the lot and into the clinic; Charlotte wants to go inside and try talking to Rebecca, to see how she's doing and to feel her anger again. She wants more yelling, more shouting, more distress—she wants a little spectacle. Anything to distract her from the crisis at hand, Olivia shivering in the hospital for who knows how long. Surely, they'd let her out within a few days? She wants to know what happened the night at the bar; did those guys do something to her? Did someone hurt her? What did you tell your therapist, Charlotte is thinking. Just let me in.

Surprising Charlotte, she does let her in. Rebecca directs Charlotte to Venmo her wife for a ride home and to get the air-conditioning going in the car; she's never requested anything, Charlotte thinks, walking to the car, opening the doors. Charlotte asks Rebecca if she wants to see the dog and she says if she does, to give her a hug and say I love her, that she will never come back.

Wear this, Rebecca says, holding up the Bourgeois imitation. Keep it on.

I can't wear my seatbelt over this, Charlotte says. An airbag will ruin it if we crash. Rebecca honks the horn, says her address, promises she'll drive smooth, easy. Charlotte doesn't know the neighborhood well and has to follow every detail of the directions. Rebecca doesn't help, doesn't say anything, just pokes at Charlotte's bulbous layers and looks out the window.

Inside the house Rebecca shares with a bunch of guys Charlotte hasn't met, Rebecca asks Charlotte to come over here. She pushes out from a seat at the kitchen and waves Charlotte toward her lap. Charlotte stops at the fridge and roots around in the freezer; it's a mess, Rebecca says, suddenly all Emily Post polite, whatever you find is probably ice-burned . . . Charlotte peels back the lid on an unopened nondairy black Thai tea pint of ice cream. She sits on Rebecca and doesn't try to hold her own weight. Push me off, Charlotte is thinking. Tell me I'm too much. She's still wearing her belly.

Rebecca puts her fingers to her nose and sniffs. Then she presses a few into Charlotte's mouth. She wonders what Rebecca is thinking as her pointer finger taps her molars before settling on the permanent retainer on her bottom teeth. Rebecca kisses her temple while keeping her eyes on the opposite wall, and Charlotte notices a calendar of purebred kitties that hasn't been changed since last month. Charlotte bites her fingers but Rebecca keeps them in place. Charlotte wiggles her head away, feeling agitated; she's ruminating on the disappointment of her existence, the mistakes she makes happily and easily, a fun goofy girl on an emotional bender.

You didn't draw blood, Rebecca says. I would have let you.

I'm sorry, Charlotte says. I can never get it right. She tenses into herself and hunches her shoulders. I'm so pitiful, she's thinking. Look at me and see how sad I am. She's thinking: Ask what's making me dead inside. I dare you.

Can I do anything, Rebecca asks. Can I help?

Obliterate me, Charlotte thinks. Hold me down while I spit in your face. She tries to focus her breathing. Belly to back, she thinks. Get that stomach to touch that spine.

Charlotte presses herself down against Rebecca's legs. Push me off, she's thinking as she squares the bottoms of her feet into the floor. She's worrying about the dog and her Rebecca, about Olivia; getting what she wants, this attention, this consumption, feels hollower than she expected. She'd gotten a big show. Is this really her finish?

Rebecca tells her to keep eating the ice cream and un-
button her shorts. They're denim with a clasp at her belly
button and short, uneven leg holes. Charlotte freezes. Rebecca repeats herself and Charlotte opens her mouth: it's
full of wet black sugar. Rebecca reminds her that's not
what eating means. Charlotte swallows and lets Rebecca
take her by the forearms and turn her around. Rebecca
pulls her cutoffs down and narrates her observations
to Charlotte: she's looking out a window over the sink
where she feels sure she is making a memory. Her legs are
cold and damp behind the knees. Charlotte knocks Rebecca's head between her thighs after she bites her calves.

Sorry, she says, and she believes she means it.

Rebecca tells Charlotte not to speak with her mouth
full, didn't anyone ever teach her manners? Rebecca has
revealed a whole story she has going about Charlotte:
spoiled enough to still rely on her parents while feeling
independent, like she's a feminist who has made something of herself. You'd've been embarrassed to be seen
with me, Rebecca tells her softly. If you knew who I really
was inside.

Rebecca says Charlotte is the sort of woman who got
into sugaring to poke at the parts of herself she doesn't
understand. Avoidant, flighty. She notices the stretch
marks on Charlotte's outer thighs and kisses them while
Charlotte imagines recording calories in a fitness app,
hating herself. Rebecca is going down on her from behind, her tongue entering her vaginal canal with her
underwear still on, the wet cotton, she knows from experience, an odd sensation but not a bad one, and she is

saying her usual quiet requests, and then Charlotte says she doesn't deserve this, she doesn't deserve any of this.

Hey, Rebecca says quietly. For you.

With the breast pump in hand, Charlotte nuzzles Rebecca and lays out her scene. Olivia and Bea and her wife and the hitting. And she's here in a house with bathrooms with moldy curtains and three-in-one shampoo. How?

It scares me, Rebecca says.

What part, Charlotte says. She, too, sounds afraid.

Everything about us, she says. How we can be real people who are really doing these things.

Let's not be real, Charlotte says, and she air-slices both their hands off.

Her scene, as she explains it to Rebecca, has to feel like she's too tired to do one more thing. I'm at the end of my rope, she says, giggling and trying to frown. I don't know how women do it all. She goes on about her exhaustion, the less-than-satisfactory student evaluations and how frustrated her parents are she hasn't gotten tenure in the art department yet, and Rebecca prepares the pump. She doesn't sanitize it or even rinse it under the faucet. Charlotte talks about how hard it is to have a five-month-old and be back in the classroom, the relentless emails all *Just following up?* and Rebecca directs her to straighten her spine and roll her shoulders back. Her feet aren't flat on the floor, the whole setup could be better, but Rebecca works her nipple in and it gets stuck in the flange tunnel and she thinks, Oh fuck, and Charlotte moans.

You're a dream, she tells Rebecca but she keeps her

eyes open, watches her pump. Rebecca is nervous, awkward, and Charlotte sees it as well as she sees anything else: the open cereal boxes, the dishes in the sink. Grease stains beside and behind a possibly broken stove. They see each other as dull-skinned in the face and in general, pasty more than pale, and in worse lights, the circles under their eyes could read as bruises. They regard each other as sick women doing sick things. Next, she says, and like a good line worker, Rebecca acquiesces.

Charlotte's nipples redden fast. Charlotte's skin is very angry.

You're going to flake up, Rebecca says quietly. You're going to hate me tomorrow. Charlotte makes noises and grinds against Rebecca's legs; the ointments and lotions and flaking skin are the point, all that aftercare.

Are you touching yourself, Rebecca says. Charlotte tells her no. Are you thinking about it, Rebecca asks, and Charlotte says she's thinking about dying.

Together, Charlotte says. Like this.

Rebecca jolts up and says she has to piss, but she looks unsteady on her feet. The world feels cool and sprinkled to Charlotte, like the first hit from anything or anyone you love. Charlotte says she needs to reset her life, to mold it from a different beginning. Rebecca tells Charlotte she'd give a lot to never live again.

In the morning, Rebecca and the sweaters are gone. On a Post-it, she wrote: *tell Olivia you notice everything, you'd miss everything, you already miss everything (I know you're looking, she doesn't!!)* —R

33

A BABY MAKES A NOISE IN THE LOBBY. NO, IT ISN'T a baby. It's a bigger baby. A toddler, I think. We're waiting for the custodian to finish mopping up water outside the single unisex bathroom on the first floor. A sign on thin printer paper says it is NOT RUNNING RIGHT NOW and I wonder how long it's been up but I can't quite establish a timeline of my own life. Bea's been home for a few days. We've been feeding her boiled chicken breast and brown rice. My wife and I have decided not to discuss the last few months at all.

That's why I'm back in this government office building waiting to piss and then go upstairs. I don't need to piss that bad. But this woman, this mother, I guess, is familiar to me. I can't look away from her. She's frowning even when her face is neutral. I want to anger her.

My partner and I had to reschedule our last appointment, I say. She jumps a little; she didn't expect me to speak and I can't blame her. We haven't made eye contact because I've been staring at my dirty feet—I've been wearing dollar store flip-flops around the city again, trying to remind myself I can survive with even less than what I've had.

That's nice, she says. It's great they're flexible.

A friend was having an emergency, I continue. So we had to like, send the social worker home. And I'm here to follow up on our baby placement.

You already have a placement, she says. Really? She seems to assess me. I can hear her thinking: But how?

Oh, I say, as though it's casual and as though it's true. Yeah.

How old, the woman says. Her eyes are hard now; I wonder if she's been rejected. I almost tell her she doesn't seem the type to open her home. I tell her it's a baby but we're trying to keep details private and she nods as though this makes a special kind of sense.

We're sticking our toes in, she says. I don't say anything and she adds that this little guy is her first baby, a gift from IVF, and now she and her husband are ready to do the foster-to-adopt pipeline. We're ready to give back, she says, then laughs.

What if the family wants the baby back, I say. I've never asked my wife this or even myself.

Well, that would be great, she says quickly. I mean, that's why the department is so involved, right? To help us navigate these decisions. She glances to the janitor;

he's still mopping. The building is quiet except for the sound of air-conditioning.

Loud in here, she says. Isn't it?

How old is your kid, I ask. I can't tell if it's really a baby or more of a toddler. I don't know what age that shift in identity happens. I want to ask the woman if the kid has developed kneecaps yet—I read online once babies have just the joint, no protective shell—but I don't want her to call the police. Instead I add that the baby seems content and she releases a groan.

I don't know, she says. I stopped tracking months.

Wow, I say, meaning it for once. That's cool.

I'm sorry, she says. I'm really tired. I don't say anything but I nod and she continues. She tells me she's exhausted and she wishes she wasn't even doing these training sessions but she really wants another baby before she's too old. She shares she was an only child and look how she turned out. I don't have any help, she says. No sister to fly in and stay with me.

That sounds hard, I say. I think I am doing a great job at being kind.

I can't even piss in peace, she says, still staring at the baby's bare feet. I hope the baby doesn't know how she feels.

We're all here now, I tell her. If you want to use the bathroom.

The woman looks at me as though I am the smartest person she has ever seen. She looks around and reality backs me up—there are, in fact, people all around. Not right beside us, no; that's just me and our mopping friend. But in offices, sure. There must be security some-where. The woman says it can't be that much longer for the bathroom and I tell her to go upstairs; it's down the hall from the room with the shitty AC, I tell her, and she laughs, comforted, I guess, at my familiarity with the building. There is no particularly shitty AC, but she doesn't know that.

I can't manage the stroller on the stairs, she tells me. It's just not worth it.

Leave the baby, I tell her. I'll help.

We look at one another for a long time. She asks me if I'm sure I don't mind staying here just for a minute and I say, Take as long as you need, and we're real chummy. I realize where I know her, then: it's bulk nuts spit-up. Not because of her face or voice but because of her mauve workout outfit. Something in the angry way she moves in it. I want to tell her I never forget a customer whose soul I understand.

In my white blouse, I am camouflaged. I dressed up real nice to come and plead my case; the reality is, our caseworker hasn't replied to our voicemails or emails. This silence might be normal and it might not be. Re-gardless, my former customer doesn't recognize me. Not even a flicker. Take as many minutes as you need, I tell her. I don't mind.

Really, she says. You're sure?

She tells me the baby's name and I forget it immedi-ately. I won't need it.

34

REBECCA SETTLES INTO GRADING. THE PLEASURE she gets in reading the work her students turn in embarrasses her; she didn't go into academia because she perceived herself as particularly kind or supportive but because she wanted the space to be smart. To justify all-nighters on subjects seemingly so esoteric to those outside her small circle of friends and rivals. People in her life stopped asking about her schedule, stopped pointing out their concerns. Is all this moving really necessary, her parents pressed. Always a different apartment, a different city. She insisted she wanted more than the consistency of corporate America. When friends wondered why Rebecca was distant then available, listless then lively, she talked about 2:00 a.m. cigarette breaks and the cutthroat inner workings of fellowship applications each winter. Her drinking leveled her, soothed her. Her drinking warmed the bad feelings until they humored her.

Her wife, for a while, was the warmth. Before her, she was drinking. After her, she was drinking. During her, she wasn't drinking and then she was and then she stopped and then she started and then she hid and then she was discovered. Rebecca's betrayal sat deep. They had never been less than entwined—no boundaries, no limits in direction of bliss or depression. Rebecca knew things were getting bad, then worse. Her drinking scared even her; of course it scared her wife. She wasn't sure how exactly she was going to get better; she didn't think she could commit to sobriety, and wanted doing only wine or not drinking before noon to be enough. She thought functional alcoholism had an unfairly maligned reputation. But she wouldn't be alone; Rebecca would drop and bounce with her. She didn't want her wife to be unhappy, exactly; she thought they'd be happier when her problems were solved, or at least when they were focusing on someone else's problems. She was the biggest fuckup for a while longer than she might have liked, but she didn't actually expect Rebecca to leave. Or to stay gone.

Bea barks.

Rebecca opens the door and sees a homely baby. The baby's blank face conceals her wife's expression as she holds him up like a trophy or a shield.

Welcome home, she says, and the family goes inside.

ACKNOWLEDGMENTS

I received an offer for *Sweetener* on October 11, 2023. In the eighteen months since, more than fifty thousand Palestinians have been killed in Israel's long-waged war on Gaza. More than one hundred thousand Palestinians have been injured. Almost all are living with food insecurity and lack access to clean water, health care, and education. Republicans are working hard to criminalize queerness, with trans people (and especially queer and trans youth) under targeted attack. Moms for Liberty and conservative groups like it are mobilizing to demonize books by and about marginalized people and defund libraries. Conservatives are *still* going after free lunch and food stamps, two programs I grew up on. Luck and privilege allow me time to think, read, and write my stories.

For all who have held my heart in the making (and living) of this book, you know who you are, and thank you.

From the river to the sea, Palestine will be free.

Marissa Higgins (she/her/hers) is a lesbian writer. She is the author of the novel *A Good Happy Girl*.